Dear Reader,

We're expecting! American Romance is proud to announce our New Arrivals subseries. This spring, some very special authors are inviting you to read about equally special heroines—all of whom are on a nine-month adventure! We expect each soon-to-be mom will find the man of her dreams—and a daddy in the bargain.

This month delivers: *Baby by Chance* by Elda Minger.

Our spicy heroine, Cinnamon Roberts, gets more than she bargained for from a hypnotherapist and a sexy cowboy named Chance Devereux, in this madcap romance from one of our bestselling authors.

Don't miss another New Arrivals coming in June. Look for the New Arrivals logo—and help welcome American Romance's new baby boom!

Sincerely,

Debra Matteucci
Senior Editor & Editorial Coordinator
American Romance & Intrigue

ABOUT THE AUTHOR

A gypsy at heart, Elda Minger has lived
throughout the United States and Europe. She
currently enjoys life in Palm Springs, California.
When she's not writing, she's usually either
gardening, dreaming, fooling around or at
the movies.

Books by Elda Minger

HARLEQUIN AMERICAN ROMANCE
117—SEIZE THE FIRE
133—BACHELOR MOTHER
162—BILLION-DOLLAR BABY
229—NOTHING IN COMMON
314—WEDDING OF THE YEAR
388—SPIKE IS MISSING
469—BRIDE FOR A NIGHT
489—DADDY'S LITTLE DIVIDEND
531—TEDDY BEAR HEIR

Elda Minger

BABY BY CHANCE

Harlequin Books

TORONTO • NEW YORK • LONDON
AMSTERDAM • PARIS • SYDNEY • HAMBURG
STOCKHOLM • ATHENS • TOKYO • MILAN
MADRID • WARSAW • BUDAPEST • AUCKLAND

To Betsy Smouse, who deserves a romance all her own.

ISBN 0-373-16584-6

BABY BY CHANCE

Chapter One

Cinnamon Roberts knew that Tuesday afternoon, March 16, of her thirty-first year on Earth, was the day that her life had started going to hell.

But on that particular Tuesday morning, she had no idea what was about to happen, so she blithely got on with her own life, and that life's grand passion—meddling in her twin's business.

That twin, Pepper, was currently slumped back on her sofa, crying her eyes out.

"He's going to—going to leave me," she snuffled out between sobs. "I know it, I can feel it—"

"He is not! He's nuts about you!"

"Not if—not if I can't give him a ba-ba—"

Baby. She can't even say the word, Cinnamon thought as she sat next to her twin sister and held her hand. There was no possible comfort she could offer her twin that she hadn't already tried in the last few months.

Pepper was married to Luca Corsino, an Italian Stallion through and through. They'd been madly in love when they'd eloped six years ago, and had put off having a family in order to bask in the glow of their incendiary passion.

Now, heading straight toward the seven-year itch, Luca wanted a child. Pepper wanted a child. They'd been trying for months, with no results. Really *trying* trying. Not just fooling around.

No saunas or hot tubs for Luca, and he wore the prerequisite pairs of boxer shorts. Pepper took her temperature religiously each morning, and Luca ran home from work at every opportunity for conception. Elevated hips, hopes and prayers, the works.

And nothing had come of it.

Pepper's soft sobs sounded loud in the sunny living room. As Cinnamon glanced around the friendly, pastel-hued room, she almost succumbed to her own fears for her sister.

What if something was truly wrong with her in the baby-making department?

Luca, devoted Daddy-to-be that he was, had already had his sperm count checked, and he was ready to go, millions of the little things waiting for the chance to score a biological touchdown.

Pepper hadn't yet gotten up her nerve to make an appointment with a fertility specialist. And Cinnamon understood that reaction, as she was the master procrastinator of all time.

This was part of the reason her life was in the mess that it was, but that mess had to be put on hold while she figured out a way to help her sister get past her pain and fear.

Would her brother-in-law leave if Pepper couldn't give him the baby he wanted? He'd wanted to start trying before Pepper had, and as Cinnamon stared at her sister's bent head, she wondered if he blamed her for that.

She swallowed against the tight lump in her throat. If, God forbid, her sister could never have a child, would Luca still want her?

He'd wanted Pepper badly when he'd chased her all over Las Vegas. Their courtship had been as unorthodox as possible, down to their wedding at the Little Chapel at the Glen.

Still holding her sister's hand, she bowed her head.

I need some help here. Oh, I know I've been asking you for guidance about what to do with my own life, but can we put that one on hold for a while? How about something for my sister? I can't stand to see her in such pain. Can't you give me a sign, a little nudge, an indication of the direction I should take?

The doorbell rang.

A definite sign, Cinnamon thought.

She let go of her sister's cool, trembling hand, got up off the sofa and walked toward the front door of the spacious town house.

The woman standing at the door defied description.

Her hair fell to her waist, long and blond and lush. Her ears were pierced with as many holes as the lobes would allow, and a dazzling array of crystals adorned her ears, wrists, neck and even an ankle bracelet that peeped out from beneath a garishly rainbow-hued caftan.

She looked exactly like Peggy Lipton in a New Age mood.

"Hey, Pep! You ready to go?"

A common-enough mistake, given that they were identical twins.

"I'm not Pepper. I'm her twin sister."

"Cinnamon! Oh, she talks about you all the time." The woman reached out for her hand and shook it vigorously. "Did your mother have stock in McCormick Schilling?"

She thought she'd heard it all before, but this was an original approach. "Nope. She was just overwhelmed by this." As she spoke, Cinnamon fingered a strand of her vivid, dark red hair.

The woman laughed. "I would've been a little overwhelmed, too. I'm Deva. Is your sister home?"

"She is, but she's—not feeling too good right now."

"Hmm." Compassion warred with practicality in the young woman's features. "She must've forgotten our appointment."

"With a fertility specialist?"

Deva sniffed, tossed her blond head and gave her a look. "No. With Madame Babala from Hungary, the best hypnotist Las Vegas has to offer."

When Cinnamon didn't answer, she said, "I researched them all, and this woman gets remarkable results."

"Let me get this straight. You're taking my sister to a hypnotist to help her to conceive?"

"That's it in a nutshell."

"She knows about this?"

"She asked me to find her the best hypnotist in town."

She's going off the deep end is what she's doing. "I don't know that she's in any shape to see anyone this afternoon."

Deva's very pretty face fell. "Oh, Cinnamon—"

"Call me Cyn. Everyone else does."

"Wow. What a terrific nickname. I bet it gets a great reaction in the bars."

"It has its moments."

Deva got back on track, her crystals glinting in the strong, desert sunshine. "Cyn, she's got to go! Madame Babala is booked weeks in advance, and this was the only appointment she had free for the next few months."

Cinnamon narrowed her eyes. "This woman's really that good?"

"The best."

"You think she can help?"

"She's helped other women relax and get pregnant." Deva touched her arm, and Cyn saw sympathy in the woman's clear blue eyes. "You know that adoption syndrome? A woman adopts, then boom, she gets pregnant. Sometimes, doing something to take the pressure off helps a lot."

Cyn sighed as she thought this through.

A sign. A little nudge. A direction. Okay, I'll go with it.

She opened the door wider and Deva stepped inside.

MADAME BABALA WAS an eyeful.

She lived in a huge house on the outskirts of town, and the minute the three women entered the front door, they were assaulted with the scents of goulash, nutmeg and patchouli.

"Come, come. Do not be afraid."

"Didn't I see this same setup on *Tales from the Crypt?*" Cyn whispered. Deva shot her a look.

"Ah, so we have a skeptic in our midst."

Cyn found herself looking into the deepest, darkest eyes. The woman was beautiful, in a striking, high-cheekboned, Eastern European sort of way. She saw no condemnation in the woman's gaze, only an attempt to understand.

Suddenly she felt totally ashamed, making light of something her twin wanted to attempt.

"I'm sorry," she whispered.

"There is no need. We are all nervous when we do not understand."

She put her arm around the still-shaky Pepper and guided her into the large, sunlight-filled living room.

Cyn shot Deva a quick look of her own. "This better work."

"It will," Deva murmured, never taking her eyes off Madame Babala. "This afternoon is going to change all of our lives. I can sense it."

Cyn had no idea how profoundly true that statement was to prove to be.

"I CAN'T GO IN ALONE," Pepper whispered, grabbing Cyn's arm.

"Why? She's going to hypnotize you, not put you under Count Dracula's spell." Cyn gently disengaged her twin's fingers from the sleeve of her blouse.

"I—can't. Cyn, I'm not brave like you are."

"You married Luca. That's brave enough for me."

"Please, Cyn. Help me."

Madame Babala laid a comforting arm on Cyn's shoulder, and she jumped.

"Do not be afraid. There is no reason to be. If you would like to come in with your sister, there is no harm in that."

"Oh, I don't know. It seems like kind of a private thing—"

"Please, Cyn."

She looked into her twin's eyes and was lost. Older by exactly four minutes, Cyn had always taken the lead in their various adventures. Pepper, even though she had the more flamboyant name, had been a follower. Softer. Shyer.

And in this case, scared spitless.

Cyn could feel herself beginning to give in. "You're sure it's okay?"

"Of course," said Madame Babala.

The woman seemed harmless enough. They'd had coffee and Hungarian pastries in her spacious living room while she had gently questioned Pepper about her desire to have a child. Those deep, dark, fathomless eyes had glistened with intense compassion, and understanding of her sister's fears.

"Let's do it."

THE ROOM MADAME BABALA used was small, and off to the side. Comfortably warm, almost womblike.

A place to be reborn, Cyn thought, then smiled at her own foolishness.

"Now," said Madame Babala, both brisk and soothing at the same time. "Cinnamon, would you like me to give you a suggestion so that you will not pick up any of the hypnosis meant for your sister?"

"Nah. I'm tough." Cyn glanced at the doorway. Pepper had gone to the bathroom, and now she rushed her next words out, not wanting her twin to hear them.

"I have to be honest with you, I don't really believe in all this stuff. I'm just here because I love my sister."

"I understand."

"I want her to be happy."

"I see."

"If getting hypnotized and thinking that will help her make a baby makes her happy, then I'm all for it."

Madame Babala nodded her head. "Still, I would suggest that you let me—"

"No. Really. I'll be fine."

Those dark eyes studied her for a long moment, and Cyn fought the urge to squirm.

"Then know that I am here for you, should you ever need me."

"Sure thing."

Another long look. "Sometimes, Cinnamon, we cannot stop people from racing toward their destinies."

"Tell me about it."

Then Pepper entered the room and the session began.

"DOES YOUR HUSBAND HAVE a pet name for you? Something that would only be said in the privacy of your bedroom."

Cyn closed her eyes. This was getting to be a little embarrassing. The last thing she wanted to know was anything about Luca between the sheets.

Pepper hesitated, then said softly, "He calls me his hot little cayenne pepper."

How appropriate for a chef, Cyn thought. Her eyelids fluttered shut, and she opened them with a start. The room was so warm, it was beginning to get to her.

"Then when he says the word *cayenne,* you will turn into a warm and willing relaxed woman who has one thing on her mind—getting this man into bed and making a child with him. Hours and hours of glorious, passionate lovemaking."

"Okay." Pepper's voice sounded so very small.

Madame Babala smiled, exposing perfect teeth. "There will be no shame. No inhibitions. Anything possible between a man and a woman will be explored, with no hesitation. Your desire will bloom, overwhelming you. The utmost thought in your mind will be to relax, to enjoy, to let nature take its wise course...."

"Madame Babala?" Pepper sounded like a nervous little girl addressing a rather formidable teacher.

"Yes?"

When Pepper hesitated, the Hungarian hypnotist touched her hand gently and said, "Please, my dear, tell me what is troubling you so that I might help."

"It's just that—I'm a little self-conscious about sex and I'm not sure I'll be—comfortable remembering all this stuff that Luca and I should do."

"And this makes you nervous, and then you have more trouble getting pregnant. I see. Well, I'll also put in a suggestion that you will forget everything that happens between you and your man on the night you make love. You will have no idea what happened, thus you will remain relaxed and comfortable afterward. You will have absolutely no anxiety. Then once you are pregnant, you can visit me one more time and I will take the suggestion out of your mind. All right?"

"That would be wonderful," Pepper breathed.

Cyn watched as her younger sister seemed to visibly relax, go under the hypnotist's soothing influence, and take in Madame Babala's soft, trancelike words. It hurt to see her sister put so much faith and trust into this

New Age mumbo jumbo. It hurt to know she was so vulnerable she would try almost anything.

But if it helped, even if only in calming Pepper's agitated mind, who was she to judge?

Well, my work here is done. Cyn had chosen a comfy, overstuffed chair behind the Hungarian hypnotist, and now she let her eyelids flutter shut. It had been an exhausting morning, from the moment Pepper had called her, sobbing, through comforting her and finally ensuring she made this appointment.

As Cyn drifted off to sleep, she heard Madame Babala's soothing voice.

"Cayenne..."

"YOU'LL SEE IF IT WORKS tonight," Deva predicted, a wicked grin on her face.

The three of them were sitting in Pepper's kitchen as she fixed them each tall glasses of iced tea.

"What did you think of her, Cyn?" Pepper asked.

That she was a fraud. But she couldn't hurt her sister by voicing her opinion out loud.

"It was pretty intense."

That was noncommittal enough.

Pepper smiled at her, but Cyn could see she didn't fool Deva. Later, as the two of them walked toward their respective cars, Deva called her on it.

"I don't want you to think that I'm trying to offer your sister false hope. Or hurt her in any way."

"I don't believe that, Deva. It's just—hypnosis?"

"Stranger things have worked. Don't you ever watch 'The X Files'?"

"I don't believe any of that stuff."

Deva paused, about to insert her car keys into the lock. "Really?"

"Really. I got a real hard lesson in reality from my Dad."

Deva's expression softened. "I know. Pepper told me how things were while you guys were growing up. It must have been tough."

You don't know the half of it. "It was."

Deva hesitated. "You were a great older sister, Cyn. She still thinks the world of you."

"I know." Cyn hesitated. "Even though I don't believe in all that hypnosis stuff, I couldn't let her down. But sometimes—hope can kill, you know?"

Deva nodded her head, then turned and unlocked her car door. Cyn did the same, and soon she was out on the city streets, heading for home.

CHANCE DEVEREUX HAD BLOWN into town on a mission. He had some bull semen to buy in the next week, but in the meantime, finding himself stranded in Las Vegas waiting for the breeder was not the most painful of life's situations.

He'd played the slots and won, tried his hand at blackjack and lost, and now, showered and shaved and with a king-size buffet beneath his belt, he was ready to raise a little hell.

He was ready for a woman.

A nice, willing, uncomplicated woman. A woman who could make him forget all the work he'd put into his ranch, and how close he was to finally realizing his dream.

Bull semen might not seem like a big deal to most people. In fact, it might even seem downright gross. But to a rancher and cattle breeder who was about to have a chance to impregnate some of his finest cows with the genetic endowment from one of the greatest champions of all time, well, this was as big a deal as it got.

"Hey, babe." A hooker in a screamingly loud lime green spandex minidress gave him the once-over.

He onced her over in return, his tired brain kicking into gear as he wondered whether she was wearing any underwear.

In that getup, not likely.

"Hey, good lookin'!" he called back, and she laughed and tossed her head, causing her long blond hair to ripple over her shoulders.

"You waiting for someone?" she asked.

He nodded his head. There was no use hurting this little gal's feelings, but she just didn't do it for him. He'd always had a thing for redheads, the wilder and hotter the better. And tonight, he had a feeling he was going to get lucky—and laid—in that order.

No messy attachments. No emotional females to placate. No families to mollify. He was this close to his dream, and he didn't want anyone—specifically, any *female*—to mess things up.

Annie had tried, God love her. He'd been mad about her, but she'd fought to change him from the moment the preacher had pronounced them man and wife. He liked jeans and boots, she wanted a city boy in a suit. He liked chili, she wanted champagne.

The only place they'd clicked was in the bedroom, and it hadn't been enough to make their marriage work.

During the divorce, she'd tried to destroy him by taking away the thing he'd loved most. His ranch.

He'd lost big, and started over. But she hadn't broken him then, and no woman was going to break him now. He was just a little more discriminating in the lust department, and tried to lead himself with his brains and not his branding iron.

It didn't take him long to find the bar he sought, and he laughed out loud when he saw its name.

The Branding Iron.

A garish sign depicted a neon cowboy kneeling over a neon cow on its side. The branding iron moved back and forth, back and forth, as the cowboy got the job done, branding this particular cow well into eternity.

Strains of country and western music emanated from the bar, and the smell of hot and spicy food wafted out into the night. Bursts of laughter made the excitement in the air almost palpable.

The bar was right on the strip, in the middle of the action. The place was packed with warm bodies, the women looked beautiful. Chance grinned. He'd find himself the sweetest little redhead to spend the night with and take the edge off eight long months of celibacy.

Tonight was his night.

SHE WAS TAKING A SHOWER and wondering what to do with the rest of her life.

Now that the crisis with Pepper was over—for the time being—Cyn wrapped herself up in a terry-cloth robe, threw a towel over her wet hair and wandered downstairs.

Her refrigerator was depressingly empty. She was just a typical *Cosmo* girl, with a couple of Heinekens in the fridge and a limp, brown head of lettuce. That was the trouble with having a twin who was a gourmet cook. She'd mooched more dinners off Pepper than she cared to admit.

When Luca had joined the family, a real live chef, she'd regularly spent the dinner hour with her sister and brother-in-law. But not lately, as she hadn't wanted to add to the escalating tension in their relationship.

You have to start cooking more. Hell, you have to learn to cook, period. Cyn, you've got to start making an effort. Going out. Meeting men—

She considered having a beer for dinner, then shut the fridge door. Stopping her depressing train of thought, she grabbed the remote, then turned on the television.

A perfectly coiffed reporter was standing outside a bar on the strip, talking.

"—The hottest new bar on the strip, with a phenomenal record of romance! Many young couples go directly from this watering hole to one of the many chapels this city is famous for."

Wonderful. What a compatibility test.

"Terri, what prompted you to marry Mark?"

The young blonde giggled. "He had the cutest butt."

She almost clicked off the set when the reporter's words penetrated the tired fog of her brain.

"And tonight is ladies' night, all you man-hungry gals! Free drinks for any female brave enough to face this crowd, plenty of happy hour snacks, and a door prize to the first redhead that walks through that entrance."

Her hand stilled as she took this all in.

Forget the free drinks and door prize. I want the snacks.

It had been a depressing day, and she suddenly didn't want to spend the evening alone in her town house.

What kind of food?

"—Buffalo chicken wings, fajitas, guacamole, tacos, tostitas, Texas chili—"

Sold.

She headed up the stairs without a backward glance.

HE'D HAD HIS EYE ON every single redhead who'd walked in that door, and none of them had done it for him.

You're too picky, Devereux.

Picky, hell. You're just scared.

The divorce had done that to him. Annie had just about cut his heart out and thrown it in the path of a cattle stampede. He'd walked around for months after their divorce, numb with shock and hurt. Emotionally destroyed.

Then his anger had surfaced, and he'd known he was going to make it. He'd put everything he had into the ranch, almost killing himself in a desperate attempt to make it work.

He'd lost. He'd started over.

Five years later, he was the owner of another working ranch, in partnership with his cousin. His dream, to breed championship cattle, was about to become a reality.

But in making his current dream a reality, he'd kind of neglected his physical needs. Oh, he'd fooled around with a woman now and then, but nothing on a regular basis.

A wild night with a willing woman every eight to ten months was nothing to write home about. The ranch had taken up most of his time, but deep in his heart Chance knew that wasn't the reason. He'd felt like he couldn't cope with women, with what they wanted and what they could potentially do to a man. So he'd left them alone, except for an occasional midnight encounter.

No more. He didn't want to get deeply involved with any female, but he had decided on the long drive to Las Vegas that he was going to start enjoying feminine companionship on a more regular basis. He'd deliberately come to the city a few days early, with the express intention of finding some action. Hitting the sack with the most desirable woman he could find was his top priority.

True, these were crude, masculine concepts. Totally boorish, sexist approaches to the fairer sex. He'd be honest with whatever lady he found, wouldn't promise more than he was capable of delivering. He'd never lied to a woman to get her into bed; he just didn't think he was capable in the romance and commitment department.

Annie had kind of burned it right out of him.

He didn't have any false modesty about what he could offer a woman. He was a man who lived close to nature, and came by his muscles and thoroughly masculine build through long hours of labor, not the latest bodybuilding techniques. He was earthy and sensual in a way that most people who grew up on a farm or ranch were. The human form, specifically the female form, was, in his opinion, one of God's finest creations.

He was primed and ready.

He was going to stay in complete control.

Then she walked through the doorway and one look at her brought him to his knees.

"WHERE'S THE FOOD?" Cyn asked the bouncer.

"You a natural redhead?" he asked.

"What?"

"You a natural?"

She nodded her head.

"Willing to prove it? For the door prize."

She balled her hands into fists and pressed them against the bare expanse of his hairy chest. His denim cowboy shirt was unbuttoned halfway down, and she took hold of one of his chest hairs.

"Don't mess with me," she said through gritted teeth. "I'm tired, I'm hungry, I want those snacks and I want them *now*. Where's the happy hour?" As she spoke, she tightened her grip on his chest hair.

"Over there." All thoughts of the door prize, or the state of her hair color, natural or not, had apparently fled from his mind.

"Thanks." She flashed him a quick grin and headed toward the food.

HAIR THE COLOR of a fiery sunset. Long, *long* legs to die for, and a fighting spirit.

He could already imagine her between the sheets.

He was in heaven.

He was in agony, as that very distinctly male part of his body kicked into overdrive and began sending urgent, sexist messages to his brain.

He slid off the bar stool and approached the buffet.

SHE WAS LOADING HER PLATE with food, not even caring that she had to look like a pig. She'd never had trouble burning off calories, and had always been an emotional eater. It had been an emotional day, and now she was going to finish it off with an emotional, high-fat dinner.

One that she had no hand in cooking.

"Hi."

She looked up and saw the cowboy.

"Leave me alone."

"What?"

"I said, leave me alone." Another chicken wing found its way onto her already crowded plate.

He was still standing there when she turned around, her plate held in front of her, piled high with food.

"Buy you a drink?" he asked.

She saw complete and total determination in his dark blue eyes.

"My drinks are free. Ladies' night, remember?"

"Get you one?"

She sighed. He actually was kind of handsome, in a macho cowboy sort of way. "Look, this has nothing at all to do with you. I came down here for the free food, I've had a simply horrible day, and I just want to pig out and be left alone."

"Really."

"Really."

"Well, today I got into town after a couple of really horrible years and I just want to have some fun."

The look in his blue, blue eyes left her in absolutely no doubt about what that fun entailed.

"Not with me you don't."

"Yes, with you. You're the best-looking woman who's walked into this place, and I'd consider it the highlight of my life if you'd let me get you a drink."

She studied him. Broad chest, lots of muscles. Muscles all over. This guy was as hard as a rock. He was tanned and lean and ready to go.

For a minute, she seriously considered his offer. Not the drink. The other one. The unspoken one, that had been so clear in his eyes.

Then she chickened out.

"One drink?"

"One drink."

"That's it?"

"I swear."

"Next you'll be telling me that your Mama brought you up to always respect a lady."

A hint of a grin shaded his mouth. "No, ma'am. Where I come from, we all figured it out for ourselves."

She smiled up at him. "Okay. One drink, that's it. And I get to eat my food."

"You bet."

He deftly took her plate out of her hands with one of his, put the other on the small of her back, and guided her toward a booth in a dimly lit corner of the bar.

HE COULDN'T REMEMBER enjoying an evening more. She was funny, witty, an absolute stunner. She ate like a teamster, but obviously burned it all off. He wished she'd burn it off with him, but he'd been around women long enough to know that the choice was theirs.

He wouldn't push her.

She told him absolutely nothing about herself, but he found himself telling her about the ranch, about his breeding program, about how badly he wanted the whole thing to work. She seemed genuinely interested.

"You know," she said, polishing off the last of some guacamole and tortilla chips, "you're a great guy. I mean, someone else would've spent the entire time trying to get me into bed, and here you've been the most charming companion a woman could want."

He refrained from telling her that he'd spent the entire evening thus far desperately trying to figure out an angle that might work. As determined as he was, he was finally beginning to concede defeat.

But maybe she'd agree to see him tomorrow. Maybe she'd let him take her out on a date. Maybe—

Warning bells flashed on in his mind. This was beginning to sound suspiciously like the beginnings of a relationship as opposed to a good time.

Time to end it. He had to be ruthless.

Annie. Remember Annie.

It worked.

"How about one more for the road?" he said, signaling the cocktail waitress.

"Okay." She'd pushed her plate away from her and was smiling at him. She seemed calmer now that she'd been fed, and he made a mental note of it.

What mental note? You won't be seeing her again after tonight.

They'd been sharing a pitcher of Bloody Marys, and Chance consciously refrained from asking the waitress to bring them another pitcher. One more drink for each of them, then he had to hit the road. Maybe Miss Lime Green Spandex was still in the lobby. Now, there was a gal who didn't scream commitment.

But this lady here, she was a woman who wouldn't just decide to go home with a guy and jump his bones.

He sighed, suddenly feeling old and alone. Alone and in Las Vegas, and contemplating a night of sex with a hooker. He'd never paid for it in his life.

He was sinking to new lows.

The waitress came up and he gave her the order. She took away the redhead's plate, then brought them back their drinks.

He held up his glass and made a small, heartfelt toast.

"I can't remember when I've enjoyed an evening more," he said quietly. "You're one of a kind."

She took a sip of her drink, then started to laugh. "Actually, I'm not. I have a twin sister."

His fantasy life went into overdrive, and he quickly calmed it down with an imaginary bucket of ice-cold water.

"You do?"

"Yeah."

To his horror, her eyes filled with tears, but she blinked them away and took another sip of her drink.

If there was one thing he had no idea how to handle, it was a woman in tears. Bulls, horses, cattle stampedes—these all came with the territory. Women? They baffled him.

He thought about the soap operas that Cookie watched in his kitchen, thought about the leading man and how he handled the myriad women in his life.

"Want to talk about it?" he said, taking a line directly out of their script and trying for a calm expression.

She looked so grateful it touched him.

"Thanks. No. It's—my sister, and it's kind of—private."

"I understand." He reached over and touched her hand. "I meant what I said. I can't remember when I've enjoyed an evening more than tonight." That came straight from the heart, because he was one hundred percent sure they weren't going to be doing any horizontal dirty dancing in the near future.

"That's nice." She took another sip of her drink. "They make great Bloody Marys here, you know?"

He leaned back in the booth, and, strangely enough, he was enjoying things now that the pressure was off. He'd find Miss Lime Green Spandex, and he'd think of this little redhead with her long, long legs who'd effortlessly charmed him.

"They don't. I do."

"You?"

"I took a sip of what passes for a Bloody Mary in this town and asked the bartender to fix it my way."

She laughed, then pushed a strand of dark red hair out of her eyes as she leaned closer. "So what's the secret ingredient?"

He smiled. "Cayenne pepper."

Chapter Two

"Don't move," she whispered.

"What?"

"Stay right where you are."

He stared at her, unsure of where this was heading.

She slid up out of the booth, then touched his chin with her finger. "I'll be right back," she said, then lowered her voice to a sexy purr, "with something for you."

Chance watched her as she sashayed off to the bathroom, and that was the only word for what she was doing with those hips. He smiled. Then frowned.

Something wasn't right.

He was sure of it. But then, nothing was ever right when it came to women. Chance lived an extremely masculine life out on the ranch; the only woman he and the hands saw on a day-to-day basis was Eunice, his housekeeper, and she looked like a gnarled old oak tree. Otherwise, the closest he came to a female with big brown eyes was Cindy the cow.

But even for most females, this didn't feel right.

He got up out of the booth, then leaned against the table as he considered where this was heading.

She just finished telling you what a great guy you are for not plotting to jump her bones, and now she's off to the bathroom with a come-hither smile and a promise of something spectacular when she returns....

Male instinct told him to run like hell.

Male anatomy told him to sit and wait—and hope.

He was just about to leave when she came sashaying back up, threw her arms around his neck and gave him a searing, sexual, let's *do* it kind of kiss that burned out every sensible brain cell in his head.

Male instinct flew out the window.

Male anatomy went into overdrive.

His hands closed around her waist, then slid lower, then cupped her bottom and pulled her against him so she was left in no doubt as to the state of his arousal.

She laughed softly when he broke the kiss, then kissed his ear and whispered, "Then I guess you have something for me, too."

At this point, he didn't care if she was the craziest dame to appear on "Geraldo," "Sally," "Phil" or "Oprah." He didn't care if Glenn Close had taken notes from her diary for her portrayal in *Fatal Attraction.* He didn't even care if she kept an ice pick beneath her bed à la Sharon Stone.

He'd wrestled bulls, branded cattle, rode bucking broncos. He'd even eaten a little of what passed for his own home cooking before gratefully signing on Eunice.

He'd endured floods, fires, drought, even bank-ruptcy.

One woman couldn't be that much of a problem, could she? Even if she was crazy and had mood swings like he'd never seen before, where was the harm?

Chance made his decision. He was going to take what she was so blatantly offering him and, like Scarlett O'Hara, "think about it tomorrow."

"What do you have for me?" he whispered, enjoying her flirtatious manner.

"This." She stepped back and looked at him, still holding his hand. Then she reached into her purse, pulled out a scrap of black silk and lace, and handed it to him.

He eyed the brief underwear, then glanced back at her short skirt. The knowledge that she didn't have that particular scrap of silk next to her body anymore pushed him over the brink.

"Let's get out of here," he said roughly, then tossed a handful of bills on the table, giving the waitress something like a fifty percent tip. She smiled gratefully as Chance grabbed—what was her name?—grabbed this crazy redhead's hand and headed toward the door.

THEY WENT TO HER PLACE and barely made it to the bed.

And it was the sex he'd dreamed of all his life, the sex that was found in men's magazines, fantasies, thoughts and dreams. A warm, willing, sexually insatiable woman. She was on fire for him, compliant, willing, unafraid to try anything. There was no false modesty, no hesitation, and when their bodies were finally joined together on those cool cotton sheets, it was as if he'd waited all his life to find this perfect fit, this perfect partner.

Limp, spent, satiated, *exhausted,* he glanced at the bedside clock. Almost five in the morning. They'd been going at it for hours, and still her pink-glossed nails were walking through the thicket of his chest hair.

He stilled their restless movement.

"Darlin', I don't know if I can." That he should finally have to utter those particular words told him what an extraordinary experience this night had been.

"I'm sorry."

"Don't be."

She looked beautiful to him, her red hair mussed around her shoulders, her green eyes sleepy with sensual satisfaction.

"I could give you a massage."

It sounded like heaven.

He turned over, and she straddled him, then went to work on his shoulders, his back, down the curve of his spine to the swell of his buttocks and lower still....

"I don't remember asking for a massage on that particular part of my anatomy." He was smiling into the pillow. It was covered in a jungle print, and he thought how like her the bedroom was, lush and vibrant and earthy.

"I don't remember feeling the need to ask permission," she whispered, and he felt sexual arousal take over once again as he rolled over onto his back, grabbed her, then pinned her down on the bed and began to kiss her.

HE LEFT HER SLEEPING in bed, looking absolutely adorable.

Sanity had returned when he suggested they take a shower together. Once the rush of warm water hit his chest and back, he took a long hard look at where this was going.

This woman could be a fatal attraction of the worst sort.

He toweled her off, then they shared a glass of champagne. A hopeless romantic at heart, Chance had stopped at a liquor store on the way to her town house, and been glad he had later when he discovered all she had in her fridge were a few beers and a head of lettuce that was heading toward becoming a medical specimen.

They were sharing the last few sips of champagne when the glass tipped, then spilled all over the rumpled sheets.

He took his bath towel and began to blot it up, but she stopped him.

"No, I'll change the sheets. It'll just take a minute, then you can lie down and get some rest—"

Warning bells went off in his head.

The terrible thing was, he wanted to stay with her. He never wanted to leave. He wanted to kidnap her, take her back to the ranch, keep her with him forever. The rest of his life, love and cherish, in sickness and health, and all that sort of stuff.

But not now. Not when he was so close to realizing his dream. A dream that another woman had almost completely shattered.

He helped her change the bed over her protests. He wadded up the jungle print sheets and took them down to her laundry room. He felt so guilty he even started a load of wash. Then he took her in his arms, kissed her with all the passion he was capable of, carried her back upstairs, tucked her exhausted, exquisite little body into the freshly made bed, watched her fall asleep—

And escaped.

SHE SLEPT THE ENTIRE DAY away, and awoke around early evening, every muscle in her body screaming in protest.

"Some bar," she muttered as she stumbled into the bathroom. She washed her face, attempting to get some of the grittiness out of her eyes, then grimaced as she smelled the stale champagne on the peach bath towel.

"What, now you're becoming a closet drinker?" she said to her face in the mirror. And what a face it was. Her damp hair stuck out all over her head, her eyes had bags beneath them the size of Samsonites, and she felt as if she'd been run over by a truck.

"Never, *never* again, snacks or not," she muttered as she squirted toothpaste on her brush, then vigorously went to work on her teeth. She remembered downing a few Bloody Marys, eating her way through the buffet table—and not too much else—

Her hand stilled. She stared at herself in the mirror.

Oh, my God... Did you bring someone back with you?

Spitting out what was left of the toothpaste, she ran into the bedroom and looked for something incriminating, like a pair of forgotten or misplaced men's leopard bikini briefs.

Nothing.

She went to the bed and pulled down the covers.

The sheets were pristine and fresh.

She sighed with relief, then sat down on the mattress, glancing around her bedroom for any revealing clues as to last night's activities. On the nightstand she spotted an open bottle of champagne and one glass.

"This solitary drinking has got to stop," she said, tossing the bottle into her bathroom wastebasket and rinsing out the glass. In truth, she wasn't much of a drinker, just socially, but life had been so stressful the last few months she would have believed herself capable of just about anything.

Sitting down on the edge of the bathtub, she put her face in her hands and closed her eyes.

You take six weeks off from work to get your life in order, and then act like someone in Cabaret. *Well, enough is enough.*

Wise enough not to cook when she was in such a state, she ordered in some Chinese food and ate. She did two loads of wash, then checked the messages on her answering machine. The first was a girlfriend, the second from her sister.

"I don't think it worked, Cyn. I mean—nothing happened. Luca and I—I don't know. Call me. I'm really in a bad place. . . ."

Cyn picked up the phone and dialed her sister's number. "I knew that hypnotist was a fraud," she muttered.

HE COULDN'T STOP thinking about her.

Even sitting in a bar, surrounded by gorgeous women who could've all been show girls, Chance couldn't stop thinking about—her.

The redhead.

Why hadn't he gotten her name? In the midst of passion, he hadn't thought about asking. Later, she'd whispered that it didn't matter.

It did matter. Even though he knew he was about to get into more trouble than a grizzly going after a hive of honey, he knew he had to see her again.

Even bull semen paled next to an evening like the one he'd shared with—

Damn. You've got to get her name.

He swallowed the last of his Bloody Mary and slammed the glass down on the bar, causing several of the patrons to give him a rather strange look. He glared back, feeling decidedly belligerent, and they glanced away.

Ah, to hell with it. You're a goner. Might as well see it through to the end....

He picked up his keys and headed toward his truck. One thing he was good at was directions. It would take him no time at all to find her house, fall down on his knees in front of her and ruin what was left of his life.

"SO YOU WERE HERE last night?" Cyn said worriedly, reaching for a stale Dorito. She was sitting on the couch in her living room, watching CNN without the sound and talking to her twin on the phone.

"For a while. Oh, Cyn, I just couldn't stay home. Not after that hypnotic suggestion didn't work. I told you that I told Luca about the hypnotist and he—I could tell that no matter how supportive he sounded, he thought I was nuts—"

"Wait, wait. Hold on. Remember what the therapist said about both of us having these hyperactive imaginations? You should just ask him what he feels—"

"I can't! What if he tells me that—"

"Damn it, he's not going to leave you over a baby—"

"But he's Italian!"

"He's also a terrific guy and—"

The doorbell rang and Cyn glanced at the front door as she chewed on a nail. There went another manicure. Stress like this was hell on her budget.

"Someone's at the door. Are you okay? I can be there in five minutes—"

"No, no, I'm fine. Just call me back when whoever it is leaves. Are you expecting anyone?"

"Nope."

The doorbell rang again, rather insistently.

"I'll call you right back."

"Cyn, I'm serious. I'm going to do whatever it takes to give Luca the baby he wants."

"I know. I'll call you back—"

Cyn hung up the phone, then raced for the door.

HE STOOD IN THE DOORWAY, rehearsing what he was about to say.

Thank you for the most wonderful night of my life. Good, good, that's a beginning.

What say we do it again? No, no, that wasn't right.

How can I begin to tell you what last night meant to me? That was better.

Something like what we had last night comes along once in a lifetime.... Even better.

He glanced down at his scuffed cowboy boots and knew he was doomed.

Ah, hell.

I can't live without you and I'm going to camp out on your doorstep until you agree to come back to the ranch with me.

The door flew open and there she was, absolutely adorable in grey sweatpants, a pink T-shirt with a pair of dice on the front, her glorious hair pulled back in a ponytail, her feet bare. Her toenails were painted a vivid pink.

"Hi," he said softly, suddenly at a loss for words.

"Hi," she said back. "Can I help you?"

He was absolutely gorgeous, and she immediately thought that her girlfriend Abby was up to her old matchmaking tricks.

Utter silence on his end made her ask the question again.

"Can I help you?"

"About last night," he began.

"Yes?"

"Could I come in?"

"I don't really know you." Instead, she stepped outside and shut the door behind her.

He looked perplexed, and for the briefest of moments, she felt truly sorry for him.

Then she figured it out. It had happened to her and her sister so many times that it was second nature to her to assume what had happened.

"I'm sorry, I really don't know who you are. But I'll bet you know my twin sister."

Relief washed through him. She'd said that she and her twin were close, so undoubtedly they were in and out of each other's houses. This was going to be all right. If he just kept repeating that in his mind and thoughts, he could get through this.

"Yeah. I do know your twin, ah—"

"Pepper."

"Pepper. And you're—"

"Cinnamon. But if you're a friend of my sister's, you can call me Cyn. Come on in."

She offered him a beer, which he gratefully took. They sat down in the living room and Cyn smiled up at him. His gut flip-flopped.

These two really were identical.

"So, how did you meet my sister?"

"Ah—" He didn't want to say he'd picked her up in a bar. Even for twins, there might be things Pepper didn't want her twin to know.

"I met her in town."

"I see. And what is it that you do?"

He grinned, starting to relax. These two looked out for each other, and Cyn's question was one that many a doting mother might ask about a man who was interested in her daughter. He decided to present himself in the best possible light.

"I'm a rancher. I own my own place, and I'm in the process of breeding championship bulls."

"Oh... *Oh!* I wonder if the same conditions apply... though why she didn't just ask her gynecologist—"

"I beg your pardon?" He set his half-finished beer down on the coffee table.

"Well, you being a breeder and all, and Pepper leaving no stone unturned in her search for information—"

He had no idea what she was talking about.

"She wants to have a baby. Badly." Cyn leaned forward, and took a deep swig of her beer.

"Well, that's just fine with me, because I love her and I want to marry her."

The beer exploded past her lips and came out her nose.

Somehow, he'd been hoping for a little more favorable reaction to his announcement.

"You *what?*"

"I said I love your sister and I want to marry her."

She was dabbing at the beer all over the coffee table with her ruined T-shirt.

"When did you meet my sister?"

"Last night," he admitted, knowing how this had to sound.

"And you—did you—"

"Did we ever."

Cyn thought frantically, then remembered what her twin had said over the phone.

I'm going to do whatever it takes to give Luca the baby he wants.

"Oh, no. Oh, dear God—"

"What! Is something wrong—"

"Is something ever wrong! If her husband finds out—"

"Husband!"

"She's married!"

His world caved in around him.

"Married?" he asked weakly.

She nodded.

"Then what was she doing out in a bar, dressed like that?"

"Oh, my God." He watched as Cyn put her head in her hands and moaned. For a moment he thought she was going to pass out, and he moved next to her on the couch and put a comforting arm around her shoulder.

"Oh, God, this is horrible."

The knock on the door startled them both.

"Cyn? It's me." The voice that sounded through the door was frantic. "I need to talk to you!"

Glancing up at him, her face white and strained, she mouthed the words, *my sister.*

He started toward the door, but she grabbed his shirt and fell off the couch in her attempt to waylay him.

"No!" she whispered. "Don't open that door! If you truly love my sister, you've got to help me!" The only thought in her mind in the midst of this confusion was that she had to protect her little sister from herself and her more hysterical impulses. She'd done it all her life, and saw no reason to stop now.

Another knock sounded, more urgent this time. Chance looked down at the desperate woman on the floor, at his knees, and knew at that moment he couldn't do anything to hurt either of them.

THE FIRST THING they had to do was retrace Pepper's steps that evening.

Sort of like figuring out who was behind a murder, Cyn thought as she and Chance entered The Branding Iron. And her sister would be the main victim should Luca find out what she'd been up to in her spare time. Cyn loved her brother-in-law, but she'd also studied all three *Godfather* movies and knew what Sicilians were capable of when they were enraged.

There'd be more than horse's heads in her bed if Luca found out what secrets she and her twin were keeping from him.

She knew she was truly upset when she realized they'd been in the bar almost forty-five minutes and she hadn't even glanced at the buffet table.

"So, you first saw her when she came in that door," Cyn said. "That's weird, because I was here last night, too. But I just had a few drinks and left."

"It was that redhead promotion. It must have caught her eye. Tell me something," he said, changing the subject. "Does she love this guy?"

"Does she ever! And I think she loves him enough to go out and do something really stupid—"

The expression on his face stopped her.

"I'm sorry. I didn't think how that might sound."

"It's okay. I know what you mean."

He retraced their steps, to the back booth where they had sat and talked and laughed.

"Then toward the end of the evening, she changed. Got really . . . aggressive. Like she wouldn't take no for an answer."

"My poor sister. She's flipping out."

"So, you think she slept with me to get pregnant?"

"At this point, Chance, I think anything's possible."

"If she does get pregnant," he said, "I'll want to have a part in raising my child."

"I think it would destroy her marriage."

"Then he's not much of a guy, if he couldn't understand how a woman could be driven to do something like—what we did. Is he forcing her to have a baby?"

"No, no, it's nothing like that. She really wants to have a child."

"What about you?"

The question took her off guard.

"What about me?"

"You. And kids."

"Not for me. They're nothing but trouble."

"How'd you and your sister wind up so different?"

They'd stopped at the bar and ordered a round of drinks.

"Chance, you've got to factor in birth order. I'm exactly four minutes older than Pepper, and it makes a tremendous difference. I act like a typical oldest child, while she's the baby of the family. What about you?"

"I was an only. But I'm close to my cousin, and he's in the middle of eight." He thought about Pepper, and found that he wanted to know more about her.

"Tell me about youngest children."

"Well, she's always been a lot softer than me. Less prickly and abrasive. People love her, because she's soft and sweet and—"

"Yeah," he said, remembering as he stared into his drink.

She touched his arm. "I'm really sorry that you're caught up in all of this. I really don't want anyone to be hurt."

"Yeah, well, big surprise. My luck hasn't been the best these last few years." He told her about Annie, and the ranch, and his dream, and found that she was an absolutely stunning listener.

There's just something about her...

As they were leaving, he said, half jokingly, "Hey, Cyn, you wouldn't consider going out with me, would you?"

She smiled. "I set up some rules a long time ago, and one of them was, I never date my sister's men."

THEY EXCHANGED PHONE numbers with the promise to call each other in the morning.

Chance lay in bed all night, staring at the ceiling. Within two days, he would have the bull semen he came into town to get and would have no real reason to stay in Las Vegas.

Other than that you might be about to become a daddy.

His own father had been rather casual about parenthood. If not for his cousin, Mark, and his family, he might have never known how a happy family operated. Now, thinking about becoming a father himself, Chance knew he could never live with himself if he walked out on his own child.

Sighing, he turned over in bed and tried to sleep.

SHE CALLED HER TWIN the moment she got home.

"Where were you?" Pepper asked.

"I had to go out." Cyn thought frantically. "Abby wanted me to help her pick out a dress for that formal dinner she's attending. I was gone for about an hour."

"Oh." This seemed to appease Pepper. "Your car was in the driveway and the lights were on. I thought you might have been home and just didn't hear me."

"Not a chance." Cyn softened her tone and put her most gentle big-sister approach into effect.

"Is there anything you want to talk to me about?"

"Oh, Cyn." Pepper sounded dangerously close to tears. "I think I've really messed up my life."

"No. No, you haven't. There isn't anything you could tell me that would make me think less of you, or stop loving you, or not want to help you."

"Really?"

"Really."

"Cyn?" She was crying now. "How come you're always so smart?"

"I'm not. I get myself into all sorts of messes."

"But you always seem like—like you know what you're doing."

She laughed. "It's a brilliant facade." Her tone softened even further. "I admire you because you reach for what you want out of life with both hands, and I just sort of sit on the sidelines waiting for something to happen."

"No, you don't! You were the single most successful Realtor at the agency—"

"At work I'm a whiz. In my personal life I'm not so hot. Remember what Abby said? It would take an act of God to make me open up to a man enough to have anything like a relationship with him." She cleared her throat, suddenly feeling emotional. This was dangerous ground.

"I admire you, the way you love Luca, the way you married him and decided to create a family with him. You have more guts than I ever will."

There was a short silence on Pepper's end, then she said, "It'll happen for you, Cyn. Just hope that when it does, you don't make as big a mess of it as I have."

Chapter Three

The following morning, Chance lay in bed and wondered if he was going out of his mind. Championship bull semen was the least of his worries. He couldn't even seem to focus on why he'd come to Las Vegas in the first place. Instead, all he could do was lie among the crumpled hotel room sheets and think about the night he'd had with—Pepper.

She'd clearly tried to switch identities with her twin, but at least now he had her real name. And she had a husband. A husband she was apparently desperate to keep happy. A husband she was willing to deceive in order to give him the baby he wanted so badly.

Was there something wrong with this guy? Why hadn't they considered adoption? Why hadn't they been able to talk about it? Why had he let her go out all alone in that kind of mental state, and to a single's bar? Had he even known?

As upset as he'd been to discover she had a husband, he couldn't find it in his heart to condemn her. She had to be in a tremendous amount of pain in or-

der to take such a drastic, risky action. And the woman
he'd sat and talked with, drank Bloody Marys with,
laughed and joked with, hadn't been some cold-
hearted, manipulating bitch. She'd simply been quietly desperate.

He replayed the entire evening in his mind, trying to
focus on each detail. She'd listened to him so atten-
tively, and told him absolutely nothing about herself.
Not even her name. That had been clever. If he hadn't
been so determined to see her again, and so good with
directions, he would have never found her town house
and never seen her again.

He wondered if that was her plan, to simply find
men who looked enough like her husband, give them a
one-shot chance, and hope they would impregnate her.
Then she could go back to her husband and tell him the
baby was his.

Usually, when he thought of a woman trying a re-
productive stunt like that one, he considered her actions nothing short of cruel. But Cyn had assured him
that Pepper was one of the sweetest women on the
planet, so Chance couldn't find it in his heart to be angry with her.

At the moment, he didn't want to examine his feelings toward her too closely.

He rolled over onto his stomach and buried his face
in the pillow, wanting to shut out the world and shut
off his emotions. He had so many mixed feelings about
what he'd done. What *they'd* done. This Luca was a
fool to let a woman like Pepper get away from him.

Most men dreamed of having a night like the one they'd shared, and he'd been so besotted by their passionate encounter he'd been completely taken over by more primitive, baser emotions. He'd simply wanted to drag her back to the ranch and make her his. Lock her in his bedroom and throw away the key.

This reaction puzzled him on a gut-deep level. He'd sworn never to get involved with a woman until the C & M Ranch was so far in the black that no one could even think of taking it away from him.

Funny how one night, and one woman, could change a man so profoundly. He sighed, then punched the pillow and tried to relax.

Even though married women were off-limits to him, Chance reasoned he couldn't be that hard on himself. He hadn't known she was married. Hell, she hadn't even been wearing a ring.

The phone rang, and he was glad for the interruption. Sometimes a man could get too deeply mired in his own thoughts. As he was usually a man of action, who loved hard physical work, wrestling with all his conflicting emotions was hard work. He welcomed the respite.

It had to be Cyn, as he'd already made contact with the man whose bull was going to put his ranch on the map. She was the only person who had his phone number besides Mark, and Mark wouldn't call unless some disaster had occurred. Of course, the way his luck had been running . . .

"Hello?" His voice was husky from sleep, and he cleared his throat. "Hello?"

"It's me. Cyn. I've talked to Pepper, and I think I'm just about on the brink of making her confide in me about the affair."

The affair. He squeezed his eyes shut. He didn't like the sound of that word.

"Uh-huh."

"So, after I get her to confide in me, I'm going to tell her that she can't go on this way, and I'm going to make her see that this whole thing is doing a terrible emotional number on you."

"Yeah."

She paused, then said, "Are you okay?"

"Yeah."

"You don't sound too good."

"I've been better."

She paused again, then said, "Would you like to come over for dinner tonight? I'm a lousy cook, but I'm great at ordering in."

He had to smile at that. There was something refreshing about a woman who knew her limitations. But he wasn't really sure if he was fit company for anyone.

"I don't know. I'm kind of tired—"

"It's not even noon. You could sleep a couple more hours, then come by my place. Please?"

He hesitated.

"It's like this, Chance. I'm feeling more than a little guilty about what my sister did to you, and I'd like you to have a nice night while you're in town to make up for it."

"You're not responsible."

"I know, but—I don't know, Pepper and I are so close, I feel as if I owe you."

He smiled. She really was a nice woman. "You don't owe me a thing. But let me bring something."

"No, no, I'll just—"

"Ma'am, I insist."

She sighed. "All right. Why don't you bring the drinks?"

"What time?"

"Six. And Chance?"

"Yeah?"

"I'm really sorry about all of this."

"Hey, it's not your fault."

SHE LIKED HIM. She liked him a lot. So much so that she gave the living room of her town house more than a quick once-over, and ordered enough Chinese food to feed an army.

As she was dressing after her shower, she caught herself as she applied just a little more mascara than was necessary.

What's going on here?

She stuck the mascara wand back into its barrel, then screwed it shut, set it down and looked into the mirror, her chin in her hands. "You really like this guy," she muttered.

She glanced away from her reflection, unable to meet it. The unwritten rule for as long as she could remember was that she didn't date her sister's men, and Pepper had come to the same conclusion. Oh, they'd done all the stupid high school stuff that twins indulged in, switching dates, laughing about it later with the men in question. But they'd never poached on each other's property, and Cyn saw no reason to begin doing it now.

She studied what she was wearing. Was it too provocative for dinner at home with a male friend? She'd dressed in black leggings and a leopard print top in warm shades of gold and black. Her hair was pulled back with a scrunchie, her makeup—

She stared at herself in the mirror.

Her makeup was a little too much.

She was about to reach for a tissue when the front doorbell chimed. The food.

Without giving her motivations another thought, she raced downstairs and flung open the door. After paying the young delivery boy and tipping him generously, she arranged the Chinese food on the coffee table in front of the fireplace—

She glanced at the fire, crackling merrily in the hearth, and frowned.

So, desert nights get cold, even in March. The temperature drops, and, well, a fire also gives the place a nice welcoming air, and the scented pinecones I threw in make the place smell nice—

Give it up, Roberts.

She started pacing around her living room. The mingled scents of cinnamon and Chinese food seemed more sensual to her than ever. Perhaps she had time to throw open the windows and air the place out, race upstairs and scrub her face free of any makeup, search through her closet for the nearest approximation of a hair shirt—

Feeling a little sorry for yourself, aren't you? Here your sister has two terrific men, while you can't even seem to find one....

She stopped that line of thought immediately, horrified at being aware of the tiniest amount of envy. And fear. Pepper was worried about having a baby, but Cyn lay in bed at night and wondered if she'd ever be able to commit to a man. She had a deep distrust of the opposite sex, and her experience with them, including her father's abandonment of their small family, hadn't reinforced any good feelings about commitment.

The doorbell chimed.

She turned toward it, hesitated, then bit her lip.

It chimed again.

Oh, for God's sake, it's not as if I can't control myself when this guy's around. No matter what I look like, what I serve for dinner, or what kind of fire I have going, it's not like I'm just going to jump his bones, attack him, never give him a chance—

She marched to the door and opened it. He stood there, looking absolutely adorable. More adorable than any cowboy had the right to be. His faded blue jeans fit him to perfection, the blue shirt covered a very impressive chest. He had boots on, and a grocery bag in his hands.

"Hi." She was aware of the fact that she was very glad to see him. She couldn't seem to stop smiling, and she pictured herself with an idiotic grin on her face. Immediately, her self-confidence vanished and she turned and led the way into the kitchen.

He followed, depositing the bag on the sink.

"I thought about Chinese beer, but then decided that Bloody Marys would be just fine."

"Great. I like mine hot, how about you?" She blushed, aware of how that had to sound, then busied herself by emptying out the sack. She provided him with two large frosted mugs, then watched as he deftly filled them with ice, vodka and tomato juice. He even washed and separated leafy celery stalks for the garnish.

With a flourish, he picked up a small bottle of spice.

"How hot do you want it? A couple of shakes of cayenne?"

She started to feel dizzy and grabbed hold of the counter. Then, as she stared at his broad back, the world seemed to fade....

"HOW HOT DO YOU WANT IT?" he said, after dusting his drink with a liberal shake of the fiery pepper. He was about to turn around when he felt her hand on the front of his jeans, placed directly over the zipper.

"How hot would you like it?" she whispered, and he'd never heard a woman's voice sound more provocative.

He set the pepper down, then placed his hand over hers and moved it off his body. He took both her hands in his and held them tightly so she couldn't do any more damage.

"Pepper?"

"Whatever." She struggled slightly to get out of his grip, then snuggled against him. He tried to step back, but he was braced against the kitchen counter with no means of escape.

"Pepper, we can't do this. Now, I want you to call your sister and ask her to come over—"

Her green eyes were warm, full of a soft, sensual light. "But there's only one thing on my mind."

"Pepper, we can't do this—"

She'd moved away from him, and now pulled her leopard print top over her head, exposing the laciest bra he'd ever seen. Black. Lace. Filled to capacity.

He swallowed.

She wiggled out of her leggings faster than any female he'd ever watched undress, then she was standing in front of him in the briefest underwear known to mankind.

"Please," she whispered, placing his hand over her lace-covered breast. He could feel the rapid beating of her heart, and his own felt like it was about to jump out of his chest.

"Why are you doing this?" he whispered.

"I want to get pregnant."

He shook his head, trying to clear his mind. Which was a difficult thing to do. Reluctantly, he removed his hand from her breasts.

"What about your husband?"

"I don't have a husband."

He wondered at her mental state. Perhaps she was in a more fragile condition than he thought. Perhaps Pepper even needed psychiatric care. Eunice had told him about a movie of the week she'd seen in which a woman wanted a baby so badly she stole another woman's child right out of its stroller. Maybe Pepper was a real danger to herself. Maybe Cyn had no idea what her sister's frame of mind really was.

"Come on," he said, then he led her to the living room and sat her down on one of the overstuffed couches. He kept her wandering hands in his own as he looked down at her upturned face. Torturous memories of their night in the upstairs bedroom raced through his mind, but, as aroused as he was, he knew he had to be the strong one.

"Pepper, we can't do this. I don't want to."

"Yes, you do." Somehow her hand had escaped his, and she traced his erection lightly through his jeans with the tips of her fingers. "You really do."

He grabbed her hand. "Okay. I'll give you that. My body wants to make love to you." He swallowed. "Desperately, as a matter of fact. But we're two adults here, and we have to think of the consequences involved—"

She wasn't listening. Somehow, she'd maneuvered her hands away from his and was busily unzipping his fly.

"We have to think of the consequences, and—"

He grabbed her hands, then leaned over and pinned her to the couch with his body, trying to still her actions.

Big mistake. She pressed her scantily clad body against his, and he could feel the softness, the heat of her bare skin. He could smell her perfume, a subtle but earthy scent.

"I'm going to get up off this couch, zip up my jeans and walk out that door—"

She shifted her body so he was lying in the cradle of her opened thighs, and he could feel that most aroused part of his body pressed against bare, female skin.

He swallowed again. Hard. He didn't meet her eyes but could feel her body moving beneath his, pressing up against him. Making him want her, driving all sane thoughts completely out of his mind...

"I want your baby," she whispered, and for some reason that poignant plea made his eyes sting. God help him, he wanted that same thing, wanted to take her right on this couch, fill her with his aroused body, climax inside her, get her so pregnant with his child that she could never, ever leave him.

It shocked him. He'd come to Las Vegas as a foot-loose, free male, looking for a little uncomplicated sex to take the edge off his carnal appetites. But one look at her, and he knew it had to be forever. He had to make her his.

He didn't quite remember the exact way it happened, but suddenly he was kissing her, moving over her, pinning her firmly to the couch. She moaned deep in her throat, and that soft sound excited him even more. Her hands were moving over his body, frantically, ripping his shirt open, buttons flying, then she was pressing her lace-covered breasts against his chest.

Within seconds, he had the front fastening of her bra released and they were both naked from the waist up. His hands shook as he pulled her panties off and tossed them on the rug. She felt so good against him, her hard, aroused nipples burning into his chest. He held her so tightly he wondered she didn't cry out at the roughness of his possession.

She was beautiful, her body answering his, no hesitation in any of her movements. He was angry, so very angry, thinking of her being this way with her husband, but then he thought she couldn't, because what they were sharing was theirs alone and couldn't belong to anyone else.

Her hard, fast climax triggered his, and he pushed inside her warmth as deep as he could as his release flooded him. And afterward he held her that way, beneath him, pinned to the sofa until that aching desire seemed to seep from his body to be replaced with— guilt. And shame.

He moved off her, intending to zip up his jeans, grab his shirt and walk out of her life forever. If he truly loved her—and he was emotionally shocked, raw at the thought of how easily that word came to him—he would leave her alone and let her try to build a life with her husband. It would be the hardest thing he'd ever done in his life, walking out of hers, but it had to be done.

He looked down at her, lying on the couch. When he'd stood, she'd curled up and now lay on her side, watching him.

"Don't leave," she whispered.

He stood perfectly still, his hand on the zipper of his jeans. He looked down at her, at her beautiful face, flushed with both passion and immense satisfaction. At her dark red hair, spread out on the sofa cushions. At the soft, sensual satisfaction in her green eyes. At the flushed skin at her neck and breasts. And it made him savagely, irrationally glad that *he* was the man who had put that expression on her face. No one else.

He hesitated.

She stretched, then slid lower on the couch, her posture, her positioning, a totally sensual signal that she still wanted him. Needed him.

He closed his eyes, despising the fact that he knew he was going to stay. When he spoke, he was surprised at the roughness of his voice.

"You're going to leave him," he said.

"Yes," she whispered.

He kicked off his boots, then his jeans. He came down on top of her again, pinning her to the soft cushions of the sofa.

"I can't leave you behind," he whispered, kissing her as he spoke to her, holding her head in his hands as he kissed her, over and over.

"I don't want you to," she said.

The fire had burned low, and night had fallen outside. The room was dimly lit, but he wouldn't have cared if they were out in broad daylight, in a car, on a picnic, at a movie. He was already aroused again, and all he could think about was how much he wanted her. Loved her.

"You can't have it both ways," he whispered as he moved his attentions to her breasts. She held his head against her, and cried out as he swiftly aroused her to as mindless a state as he was approaching.

He entered her again, and this time he made sure the loving was hot and sweet and slow. He wanted to give her everything. He forced himself to make it last a long, long time, and made sure she reached fulfillment several times before he allowed himself his release.

She fell asleep with her head on his shoulder, his arm around her, a smile of sensual contentment on her face.

WITH MORNING CAME an attack of conscience.

As he looked down at her sleeping form, he knew he couldn't force her to divorce her husband. He knew from what Cyn had told him that Pepper loved Luca deeply. They'd been married almost seven years, and you didn't just throw a relationship like that away on a whim.

If he were truly self-sacrificing, he knew he had no place in her life. If he loved her, he would have to walk away, and the only way he could do that would be to leave before he ever knew whether she was pregnant with his child or not. Because once he knew, he'd never be able to leave her.

Chance looked at her sleeping face for a long time, memorizing every feature, knowing that this was going to have to last him for a long time. And he doubted he'd ever love another woman as much as he loved this one. When it hit, it hit, and all the rationalizing in the world meant absolutely nothing.

He'd sacrifice his happiness for hers, and remember what they'd shared. Hell, it was more than most people experienced in a lifetime.

He'd leave Las Vegas this evening. All his other business transactions could be conducted over the phone. There was nothing more for him here if he couldn't have her.

He kissed her only once, softly, then got up off the couch, got dressed. His shoulders were hunched against the pain as he slowly let himself out the door, locking it behind him.

SHE WOKE LATE THAT afternoon, sore in every muscle. It took Cyn a moment to get her bearings, then she glanced around the living room at the numerous cartons of Chinese food on the coffee table, at the ashes in the fireplace.

Her stomach growled. She sat up, then winced as muscles she hadn't even been aware of burned in protest. She glanced down and saw the bra and panties on the gray carpeting.

An ominous feeling assailed her, and she sat very still, trying to remember.

She couldn't. She couldn't remember a thing.

In a daze, she got up and wandered into the kitchen. Two large mugs sat on the counter, celery stick garnishes jauntily peeping over the rims. She spotted the empty jar of tomato juice on the counter, the jars of spices, the barely used bottle of Absolut.

She swallowed, and fear began to spiral through her.

Her mother had been an alcoholic, and Cyn was quite familiar with the pattern of drinking and the subsequent blackouts they created. She'd always been scrupulously disciplined about her own liquor consumption, and now she searched the kitchen garbage can, wondering if there was another bottle they'd already polished off.

There had to be a they. This time she couldn't delude herself. Two glasses, her underwear all over the rug, her clothing in a heap on the kitchen floor...

Her eyes misted over as she thought about how pathetic her emotional life was. Was that it, did she have to get drunk in order to have an abandoned sexual relationship with a man? Was she that far gone?

She swallowed again, trying to taste the sour mouth that always went with excessive drinking, but she couldn't taste anything. Her stomach growled again.

Nothing seemed to make sense. Tons of Chinese food and here she was starving. Two drinks—badly watered down drinks, now that all the ice had melted—untouched on her kitchen counter. Sore muscles and a definite, feminine ache between her legs. Her underwear strewn around the living room.

She covered her face with her hands and took a few deep breaths for good measure. She would not give in to fear and run away from life like her mother had. She'd always been the strong one, for both herself and her sister, and she wouldn't fall apart now, no matter what she had to face. No matter how terrible.

Cyn went back into the living room and sat down on the couch, drawing an afghan around her and curling inside it. She felt cold, even though the town house wasn't particularly chilly. She felt chilled to the bone at the thought of losing her grip on reality.

Maybe she was finally cracking up. The last few years had been exhausting; she'd worked as hard as she could to find some sort of financial stability in her life. Now, when she'd finally decided to take the six weeks vacation she'd built up, it seemed she was coming totally unglued.

The phone rang, and she jumped. She stared at it for a few more rings, wondering if she'd given Mr. Mystery her number.

Get a grip and get it over with.

She picked up the receiver.

"Hello?"

"Hi."

Chance. The last person she wanted to talk to. Boy, if this guy knew the problems both she and her sister were experiencing, he'd hightail it out of the state so fast they'd barely see his dust. If he knew the truth, he'd think they were both nut cases.

Pepper, having a wild affair with this cowboy because she wanted a baby so badly. And me, sleeping with strange men—

A horrible suspicion assailed her, and she drew in a sharp breath.

"Chance, what did you do last night?"

He was silent for a moment, then said quietly, "She told you, didn't she." There was a tone of utter defeat in his voice, and he didn't sound proud of himself.

Her stomach was beginning to come apart. "Tell me what happened."

"Cyn, I don't know—"

"No, tell me. Please. I'm not trying to be a busybody, I'm just—it's really important."

Slowly, reluctantly, he outlined the entire evening. Cyn's eyes filled with frightened tears as she took in her living room. Everything was as he described it, the Chinese food, the drinks he'd mixed, her clothing on the floor, and the couch, the couch, what they'd done on the couch—

She let out a very soft moan before she could stop herself.

Chance stopped in midsentence. "Are you all right?"

"No. No, I'm not all right." She swallowed hard against the painful lump in her throat. She had to ask him to do something for her, and asking for favors had never been something she was particularly good at. For one thing, she never had any faith in them being done.

"What do you need?"

It was as if his words set her free. Her teeth were chattering, she felt as if her body was totally alien to her, as if she hadn't spent thirty-one years living inside it.

"Chance, would you do something for me?"

"Tell me."

For the first time in her life, she risked leaning on someone else. It was terrifying.

"Would you come over here right away? Before you leave? I need to talk to you."

"I'll leave now." He paused. "Will you be all right until I get there?"

"No." She was dangerously close to tears again, and if her suspicions had any substance whatsoever, before the evening was up she might just indulge herself in a full-scale nervous breakdown.

"Honey? Honey, hold on. Nothing can be that bad. I'm responsible for this whole mess, and I'll help both you and your sister. Now, you hold on tight and I'll be there in fifteen minutes, tops. Can you do that for me?"

His deep, rumbling voice was like a balm to her frayed nerves. She clutched the phone like the lifeline it was. And she wondered how she was ever going to tell him the truth.

But throughout her life, she'd always faced her problems head-on, and she saw no reason to change things now.

"I'll be here. But Chance?"

"What?"

"Hurry."

Chapter Four

He arrived at the town house in record time, rang the bell, and stood impatiently outside the door while he waited for her to answer. She did, and he noticed immediately that she didn't look well. Cyn had obviously just showered. Her dark auburn hair was wet and straggly, her face freshly scrubbed and devoid of any makeup. There was a worried look in her green eyes, and she made him feel decidedly uneasy as she ushered him inside.

"I have something I have to tell you," she whispered. "A sort of confession."

The one thing Chance was absolutely sure of at that particular moment was that he would never, ever, understand women. And Cyn and her sister were certainly no exception.

"It's okay," he said, trying for a soothing tone of voice. Trying for the tone of voice he would use with skittish horses or frightened cattle. He sensed that some sort of danger was imminent, but had no idea how to prevent it.

"I think I slept with you."

"What?"

"Okay—I think—I think I might have had sex with you."

He stared at her, wondering if she were completely out of her mind.

"What do you mean, you think?" Instinctual masculine feelings—and a considerable amount of pride—rushed to the fore. "You can't remember?" He paused, knowing how that had to sound, and decided to try a gentler tactic.

"Cyn, I don't get this—how could you not remember having sex?"

She pushed her damp hair out of her face, but still couldn't quite meet his eyes. "I wake up, I'm naked on the couch and wrapped in an afghan. There's Chinese food everywhere, and my clothing is all over the place. I'm—" she turned bright pink "—I'm sore in places that don't get sore from a regular aerobics workout, and you're telling me you had sex with my sister—"

"Whoa. You were the one who said it had to be Pepper, I thought it was you from the start. I came back to this town house—"

"I know," she whispered miserably, and started to cry.

If there was one thing that panicked him more than a stampede, more than a blizzard in high country, more than a barroom brawl, it was a crying woman.

"Cyn—Cyn, listen to me a minute—"

"You don't understand!" She started to pace around the living room in an agitated manner. "Your life isn't going down the toilet with a capital T, you don't wake up wondering how you spent the last few hours—"

"Cyn, do you drink—"

"No!" She whirled on him, her expression both frustrated and angry, and he sensed her temper was almost to the breaking point.

"Okay. Okay." He held up his hands, palms toward her, in a placating gesture. "All right. So, you think we might have slept together. I know I slept with someone last night, here, in this town house. We didn't eat the Chinese food, we got right down to it—" He paused. "Do you remember any of this?"

She shook her head, her eyes swimming.

"I can't believe, if it was you, that we had the kind of sex we had and you don't remember any of it."

The look she shot him was mortified. Her face was still flushed with embarrassment, and she crossed her arms in front of her chest and turned away from him.

A thought crossed his mind, flitted into his consciousness. He couldn't push it away. It looked like he might not only be breeding prize-winning cattle this season.

"Cyn, are you—taking any precautions?"

The way her shoulders slumped gave him his answer.

"What part of your cycle are you on?"

She was crying, her shoulders shaking.

He'd never felt more helpless, but he had to do something. He crossed the room and stood behind her, putting his hands on her shoulders.

"I'm sorry," she whispered, and the two words came out on a watery little gasp. She wiped her eyes with her fingers, and he reached into his jeans pocket and extracted a clean bandanna.

"Here."

She took it, wiped her eyes, blew her nose, stuffed it into the pocket of her white shorts.

"I think we'd better go to a drugstore," he said quietly.

She merely nodded her head.

"Cyn, talk to me."

She was locked inside her town house bathroom with a home pregnancy test, and Chance waited outside the door, frustrated and tense.

"How much blood does it take?"

No answer.

He cleared his throat, suddenly worried. She seemed like she was in such a fragile state of mind, and now this.

"Cyn?"

The door opened, and she walked out of the bathroom, her back rigid, her features composed.

"I'll take care of it," she said, then sat down on the couch and stared at the ashes in the cold fireplace.

"Oh, no. We're in this together. I'm as responsible—"

"Responsible? Thanks for the noble sentiments, but I don't want to be a burden to anyone—"

"Cyn, listen to me—"

"No, you listen to me. All of my life, I've done what was expected of me, and I haven't complained—much. I just did what had to be done, you know?"

He did know. They were more alike than he could have ever guessed. Chance nodded his head, urging her to go on.

"But there were a couple of areas where I had these silly little dreams, and I'm not going to compromise them, not even for this baby."

She *was* pregnant. Something turned over in his stomach, the tension eased, and the one thing he was absolutely certain of was that he couldn't let this woman out of his life. Crazy or not, she was his, and had been from the moment she'd walked into that bar.

He took her hand.

She pulled it away.

He eased his arm around the back of the sofa, behind her.

She scootched across the pillows, out of reach.

Ornery little thing, he thought. Cookie was going to love her. Eunice would, too.

"Cyn, listen to me—"

"I'd like you to leave."

A certain coldness had descended over her, but it didn't fool him. He knew she was scared, could sense it, and knew she was trying to push him away.

"What are you going to do?" he asked.

"It's none of your concern."

He took her hand, and this time didn't let her pull away. "It is if you're planning to—"

"No." She shook her head. "No, that's not even a consideration. I'm going to have this baby, but there's no reason both of us should ruin our lives."

She wasn't thinking straight. Several of his cousins were married, and he'd heard firsthand how pregnancy could affect a woman's thinking. Chance knew he had to be strong for her. Strangely enough, there had been another pregnancy scare in his life, when he'd been in high school. That time, he'd been scared, and thankful as hell when it had been a false alarm.

Now, he felt differently. Standing outside that bathroom door, he'd wanted to stay with her no matter what the outcome of that test.

"I want you to marry me."

She stared at him as if he'd asked her to fly to the moon, then shook her head.

"You don't want to hook up with me."

"Cyn, you can't go through this alone—"

"I've been through worse. I'll be fine."

Lord, she was a prickly one. "I don't feel right about walking away—"

"That's exactly what I want you to do."

"No. I don't think that's what you want at all. What do you *really* want?"

For a moment, those green eyes looked so vulnerable. Her mouth shook, then she bit her lip and lowered her head.

"I'm a mess, Chance. You don't want me."

"What if I said I did?"

"I can't ask you to turn your whole life around—"

"Hey, it wasn't much of a life to begin with." He had his arm around her now, and she wasn't pulling away from him. He wasn't overconfident, but he had a feeling he might get his way, after all.

"Come back to my ranch with me," he whispered, then kissed the top of her head. She sighed, but didn't move any closer. "Come back and let me take care of you."

He could sense her terrible indecision, it was almost a tangible presence around them. She sighed, then stood up, her eyes swimming with tears.

"You're a good man, Chance."

Uh-oh. He knew this speech, and it was a variation on the nice-guy one. He started to protest, but she put a finger over his lips.

"I can't do this to you. It was my own fault all this happened, and I can't make you responsible. I—" She swallowed hard. "I threw myself at you, and now I have to get on with my life."

"And what if I want you in my life?"

"You're acting out of emotion."

"Hell, yes! And what's wrong with that!"

"God, Chance, we don't even know each other!"

"I think we know each other pretty damn well!"

"Sexually, sure, but there's more to a relationship than hitting the sheets."

"So you do remember?"

"No, but you've made it pretty clear what happened. And there *is* more to a relationship—"

"Seems to me that's a pretty damn good place to start."

"Chance, we have nothing in common—"

"We have a baby in common, Cyn. I want to help you raise our child. *Ours,* Cyn. Ours."

She sat quietly beside him, and he knew she was considering his offer.

"Would you give me an evening to think things over?" she asked.

"I don't know if it's a good idea for you to be alone right now."

"I'll be okay."

He sat silently for almost two minutes, then let go of her hand and stood up. "I'd feel a lot better about all this if you'd let me bunk down here on the couch. I don't think you should be alone, you've been through a lot in the past few days."

"I'll be fine."

He wanted to ask her why she didn't remember all that had happened between them, but he couldn't think of a way of phrasing it without getting her temper riled. If she'd just let him stay with her, he could slowly wear down her resistance to the idea of their sharing their lives.

In the meantime, he'd just take things a step at a time. One thing he had plenty of was patience.

"Humor me, Cyn."

She wavered for an instant, and he knew he had her. One thing he felt very strongly was that both of them had been alone for a long time. He understood that, just like he understood the quiet pain of life just not working out the way you thought it should.

If she'd just give him a chance, he'd try to make her happy.

"All right. You can sleep on the couch, but I don't want any repeats of—you know—"

"Yeah. I understand."

THEY CLEANED UP the Chinese food, throwing everything away. Chance washed the two glasses he'd used to make their drinks, then put the vodka and various spices away in her kitchen cupboard. He threw the rest of the opened bottle of tomato juice away.

She seemed uncomfortable with him, so he left her to her own devices. Cyn went upstairs and took a nap. He watched some television, then called his cousin Mark and told him he'd be delayed a few more days. Afterward, he lay down on the sofa and stretched out. Some of the tension was leaving his body, and he found himself incredibly tired.

It wasn't every day a man discovered he was about to become a father.

The strange thing was, he wasn't worried. He wanted Cyn in his life, had wanted her from the moment he'd seen her. The baby? Well, in his mind they were a package deal, and if that little one helped them get together and stay together, then that was all to the good.

Fate hadn't been kind to Chance, but he saw this new development with Cyn as a sign that his luck was turning.

He wanted her, and he loved her. Hell, Cookie had been right, the old buzzard. When it hit, it hit, and there was no rationalizing or denying it. When it was right, it was right, and now the only job he had left to do was to convince her they were meant to build a life together.

A baby on the way was powerful persuasion. Chance fell asleep with a smile on his face.

HE HEARD HER RUMMAGING through the kitchen, the soft sounds waking him out of a deep slumber. He glanced at the digital clock on the VCR.

Eleven-seventeen. He'd slept longer than he'd thought.

Well, you didn't get a hell of a lot of sleep last night. His body tightened as he remembered the night they'd spent together, but as he swung his long, denim-clad legs off the couch he reminded himself that he was here to protect her, to inspire her to trust him, not to seduce her.

Though it was a tempting thought, it had to remain a thought.

He walked into the kitchen to find her up on a chair, balancing precariously as she tried to peer into a cabinet.

"Whoa!" He strode in, plucked her off the chair and set her on the kitchen floor.

"I was just—"

"You could've fallen—"

They stared at each other for a moment, then, miraculously, she smiled.

"I was getting kind of hungry, and I thought I remembered a box of cookies I bought a while back."

He smiled down at her, liking her more and more. "We could go out and get something. Or phone in. Or I could get you something—"

"No, I don't want you to go to any trouble. Those cookies have to be here somewhere, or a can of soup or something."

"Stay there, I'll check your cabinets."

He scanned them quickly, opening and shutting the various compartments.

"Not a thing, except a can of artichoke hearts and two small cans of pineapple."

She made a face, and he almost laughed.

"We could try that Chinese place again."

She thought about that while he opened one last cabinet.

"Oh, Cyn, I put the vodka up here for you. I couldn't find any other alcohol in the house, so it's right here in the cabinet above the refrigerator. And I couldn't find your spice rack, so the celery seed, seasoned salt and cayenne are right—"

He felt her hand on his left buttock and went perfectly still. He swallowed. "Cyn?"

"Mmm?"

"Cyn." He turned around and took both her hands in his. "What's going on?"

"Make love to me."

Women.

"Cyn, we have to talk—"

"I don't want to talk—"

It crossed his mind just then that maybe there was something seriously wrong with her. And even that didn't matter. He'd deal with it, he'd help her through whatever demons she was facing. It was more than the baby they'd created, it was the fact that she touched something deep inside him, a part of him, an emotional core that he hadn't wanted touched in a long time.

"Cyn, we can't do this—" He was totally unsure as to how to proceed. Maybe she was one of those women like the ones on "Oprah" Cookie was always talking about, who led secret lives and went into complete fugue states and didn't remember from one day to the next—

She unzipped his fly.

He caught her hand.

She pressed up against him.

He caught his breath.

He kissed her, fighting for control.

"Cyn," he muttered, his lips mashed against hers.

"Mmm?"

He thought back, quickly, to their two previous nights. She'd been warm, willing, wanting to please him. Perhaps he could use that warmth and total willingness to his—to *their* advantage.

He had to get a handle on this crazy situation before it drove him totally berserk.

"Cyn?"

"Mmm? Oh, yes, just like that..."

"Cyn, listen to me for a minute. You'll do anything I want?"

"Anything. Your wish is my command."

"I want you to go upstairs and put on your prettiest dress—"

"Okay."

"And then I want you to come downstairs and we're going to go to a chapel and get married."

"Okay." She kissed him again. "Then can we make a baby?"

His eyes stung. Something was wrong with her, no doubt about it. They'd deal with it. He'd deal with it. There was nothing, in his estimation, that time and love couldn't help, and he was more than willing to give her both.

"Yeah, honey. Then we can come home and make a baby."

"Okay." She turned and headed out of the kitchen. He followed her and watched as she disappeared up the stairs.

And he wondered, while she got dressed, if he was doing the right thing. But when she came down the stairs in a white minidress and short jacket, high heels, her hair twisted up on top of her head, and when she smiled at him—

No one could have talked him out of this particular wedding.

THEY WERE MARRIED at one of Las Vegas's many all-night chapels, by a minister who looked suspiciously like Elvis.

Chance went all out, buying the deluxe package that included flowers, expensive champagne, pictures, a video and two nights at Caesar's Palace. They drove from the chapel to the luxurious hotel and checked in.

Mr. and Mrs. Chance Devereux.

The way she looked up at him, the happiness that seemed to radiate from her exquisite little body, the smiles and little kisses, the warmth... He caught jealous glances from every male who caught sight of the two of them.

Once inside the hotel room, he poured them each a flute of champagne.

She flung off her dress, and clad in the sexiest underwear he'd ever seen, sat in his lap.

He couldn't think straight. He'd never seen a bra like the one she had on. The white lace fit her like a second skin, shaping and moulding her breasts so they were pushed up and together, and presenting him with a beautiful view of generous cleavage. The garter belt was little more than a wisp of lace, her stockings silky and smooth. A tiny G-string completed the outfit, and when she'd first flung her minidress on the bed, the sight of her had caused his mouth to go dry.

They twined their arms together and drank from each other's glasses. She laughed as the bubbles tickled her nose, and Chance fell in love with her a little bit more. "Okay, honey, that's enough." He had to remember she was already pregnant, and more than a sip or two of champagne probably wasn't a good idea.

"Okay." She looked up at him, her heart in her eyes, and he felt his own melting. He reached up and unfastened the tiny scrap of lace and netting that the chapel had given them for a bridal veil, then slowly began to take the pins out of her hair.

He fingercombed it, arranged it over her shoulders, then simply looked down at her in his lap, wondering at his incredible luck at even finding such a wild, exotic woman.

"I love you, Cyn," he whispered as he bent his head and kissed her.

"I know," she whispered against his mouth. "I love you, too."

They kissed for a long time because he wanted to take things slowly for her, make it last, make it good, give her something beyond wild, passionate sex. He wanted it to mean something, to be more emotional, to create a bond between them that would last forever.

She shifted in his lap so she was straddling him, and he caught her up against him and simply held her.

"Let's go to bed," she whispered.

"Yeah." He stood up with her still in his lap, her ankles crossed behind his back, and carried her to the king-size bed. Then he set her down as if she were breakable, knelt down and removed her heels.

"Put your feet up, baby." He didn't want to tire her out. She'd looked as if she were lit from within with emotion throughout the entire ceremony, and her feelings for him had been so plainly on her face. That had been what had caused those men in the lobby and the elevator to envy him, the fact that her emotions were open and honest and so very intense. That and the fact that such emotional honesty was rare in such a cynical world.

She lay on the bed and watched him as he undressed, and he felt her possessive gaze on his body as strongly as if she'd reached out and touched him.

He lay down next to her, still wearing his underwear.

"You can take those off," she whispered, sliding across the sheets toward him. Chance thought about the video that had been taken of their short wedding ceremony, and now he wished he'd bothered to learn how to use that sort of camera and had one with him now. He didn't ever want to forget the way she looked tonight. He didn't ever think he would.

"Let's just lie next to each other for a while." It wasn't a matter of being up to the task; she aroused him to the point where it was almost painful. But he simply didn't want to make love to her right now. He wanted to hold on to this feeling of closeness. He wanted a little calm in the middle of the storm.

He'd promised to love, honor and cherish her, and now was as good a time as any to begin. He wanted to cherish her, to let her know how he felt about her, to try to make her feel happy, and safe, and loved.

"Come here," he whispered, and she slid across the sheets into his embrace.

"Happy?" he said.

"Are you?"

He nodded.

"Then I am."

Her hand drifted downward but he caught it before she reached her goal. With enough practice, he'd get pretty good at this.

She went perfectly still.

"What?" he whispered.

"I thought—I thought we were going to make love, and make a baby."

He kissed her hand and kept his arms tightly around her. Her body felt cool, and he could feel the warmth from his own slowly calming her agitation.

"We've already made a baby, Cyn."

"We have?"

The happiness in her voice was almost more than he could bear.

"We have. You're going to have a baby, so we don't have to make love tonight. We can just be close."

She turned and faced him, their heads resting on a single, king-size pillow.

"Are you happy?"

He kissed the tip of her nose. "You bet."

She smiled and her eyes drifted shut. "Then so am I."

He thought they were going to simply go to sleep until he felt the bed jiggle slightly.

"Cyn?" He'd left the bathroom light on so the room wasn't completely dark when he opened his eyes.

She was unhooking her bra.

"The lace itches," she explained, and he caught his breath as she unhooked the undergarment and flung it to the foot of the bed.

Her breasts were beautiful, and the fact that he'd had full access to them for the last two nights did nothing to shut down his libido. She stretched her arms above her head and snuggled down among the sheets.

She was completely comfortable.

He was in agony.

She rolled on her side, then sat up in bed.

"What?" he asked, his eyes closed. If he took another look at her half-naked body, he wasn't sure if he could be responsible for his actions. They would end up being more than close, he was certain of that.

"The garter belt pinches."

He could hear her unfastening her stockings, sliding off the silky garments, then wiggling out of the garter belt.

He couldn't understand his decision. They were married, she was pregnant, so where was the harm in making love? Yet he couldn't. Not with a clear conscience. There was something different about Cyn when she was in this particular mood. She was almost...*too* compliant. As if she didn't have a will of her own.

He decided to sleep on it and see where they stood in the morning.

"Chance?"

"Mmm?"

"Would you just hold me?"

"Sure."

He slid closer, enfolded her in his arms.

"Chance?" she whispered.

"Mmm?"

Her hand closed around his erection, and he jumped as if he'd walked into an electrified fence.

He tried to remove her hand, but she held firm.

"I don't want you going to bed unhappy," she whispered.

"Honey, I'm fine."

"No, you're not. You need me."

"No, I—"

"Yes, you do."

He eased her hand gently back, then kissed her on the forehead.

"Baby, I'm not in the mood."

"But you're hard as a rock."

He gritted his teeth. "I thought we might...not make love tonight."

"Is that what you want?" Her puzzlement was clear in her voice.

"Cyn." He struggled to find the words that might make her understand. "You have to admit that this whole thing has been a little...strange."

She propped herself up on one elbow and looked down at him, unconsciously giving him an incredible view of her breasts. He swallowed.

"Anyway, I thought that, since we've already been through so much, we might want to simply rest tonight."

"But we're married. You're my husband. I'm supposed to please you."

He swallowed again, as images of her particular way of pleasing him assaulted his senses. "I know. But I thought you might want to rest."

"But the minister said, with thy body I thee worship."

He cleared his throat, wondering if perhaps a cold shower was the answer.

"Cyn. I love you and I want to do what's best for you, and I can't do that when you question me at every turn."

She nodded her head as if she understood, but he wasn't sure she did.

"Now, we've started this marriage off tonight, and I want to make things work, and I want you to be happy."

"Making love to you would make me happy."

Sweat popped out on his brow. Why was he making this so damn difficult? They were married, she was already pregnant, warm and willing, and he had an erection so powerful it had the potential to cause brain damage.

So what was holding him back?

Chance had always relied on his instincts, and his instincts were telling him something still wasn't right. Cyn had been warm and willing before, then turned into a frightened, cornered woman.

She was willing now, but how would she feel about this whole thing in the morning? He'd always heard that it was a woman's prerogative to change her mind, but Cyn made that simple action into a fine art.

"Okay," he whispered, giving her a quick hug. "For tonight, let's go with this. I'm the husband here, and I'm in charge. Just for tonight."

"Oh, no. I want you to be in charge all the time."

"What do you mean?"

"I want to do everything in my power to please you. You're the boss."

He closed his eyes briefly. "Good. So you'll agree with me if I say that I think we should use tonight to get . . . closer."

"But we can't get any closer than—" She stopped. "No, you're right. We'll do what you want. Okay." She leaned over him and gave him a kiss that almost caused his brain to short-circuit. The smell of her hair, the feel of her full breasts crushed against his chest, the silky heat between her thighs—

He was losing his mind.

She lay down beside him and they were silent for a few minutes before he heard the sheets rustling.

"Cyn?"

"I'm sorry, it's just that this lace itches—"

He thought of that tiny scrap of silk and lace being removed, leaving her totally naked in his bed, next to him. His imagination and his erection went into total overdrive simultaneously.

"Cyn?" he whispered hoarsely.

"Mmm?"

"Leave your panties on, okay?"

"Anything you want."

He knew the exact moment she fell asleep, knew by her deep, regular breathing. He, however, felt as if he'd never sleep again.

He sighed, and turned over on his side, facing her.

He tried to sleep and couldn't. For the next few hours, he simply stared at the ceiling and thought. He got up and took a cold shower, then turned off the bathroom light and plunged their suite into complete darkness. Maybe it would be easier if he couldn't see her.

She sighed in her sleep, and stretched. Her foot came into contact with his, making him even more aware of her presence.

He thought about making love to her.

He quashed the thought.

He replayed everything about Cyn, from the moment he'd met her in the bar to their wedding tonight.

He wondered if she had multiple personalities, like on "Geraldo."

She sighed again and melted back against him, her bare hip pressing against his arousal.

He gritted his teeth.

She snuggled closer.

Even though they were married, he felt as if he'd be taking advantage.

She moved against him again.

He remembered how her breast felt in the palm of his hand, so full and hot and soft—

He touched her shoulder in the darkness and she pressed even closer against him. He touched her breast, shaped the firm flesh with his hand, plucked at the nipple with his fingers. It pebbled instantly, so hard against his palm.

He thought about taking his hand away, and couldn't. He smoothed his fingers over her side, down the curve of her hip, until one finger rested beneath the lacy elastic of that small scrap of underwear, the only thing standing between him and total, fulfilling, hot, mindless sex.

He'd wanted to show her how much he cherished her, and instead couldn't seem to get away from how much he wanted her.

He slipped his hand over her belly, his fingers beneath the white lace that covered her feminine mound. Lower still, until he found that hot, slick heat.

She moaned, and moved her legs. Restless. Wanting.

You need me.

God help him, he did. He couldn't help himself. He felt like a drowning man, finally letting the water take him under. Hooking his fingers in the lacy elastic, he eased the G-string down her long legs and pushed it to the foot of the bed.

SHE WAS HAVING the most erotic dream of her life.

Probably because she'd gone without even a pitiful excuse for a sex life for longer than she cared to admit.

Oh, there had been a few men. None too impressive, though. Hell, she hadn't even been able to remember Chance, so how impressive could he have been?

But this man, *this* man who touched her so exquisitely in her dreams, was perfection.

She felt his large, warm hand on her breast, shaping it, touching it gently. And because she was deep asleep, and it was such a beautiful dream, she allowed herself to respond. His touch felt so good; he was incredibly gentle and erotic at the same time. She felt safe and sexy, warm and cared for.

His hand moved lower, over her hip, played with the elastic of her panties. She bit her lip against the powerful feeling of erotic anticipation, and knew she would let him do whatever he wanted.

Then he did what she wanted him to do, slid his hand beneath the silk and lace scrap that covered her, cupped her, felt her.

She moaned, and moved her legs. Restless. Wanting.

She couldn't help herself. She felt as if she were finally surrendering to impulses she'd hidden away inside herself all her life. She lifted her hips as he eased the elastic down her legs, pushed her panties down to the foot of the bed.

Then he was rolling her onto her back, sliding between her thighs, and she felt him, hard and hot and huge, against her skin before he parted her thighs farther and pushed inside.

Her eyes flew open as she started to climax.

The room was dark, she didn't know where she was, and this was a real man, no dream, never a dream. He was moving against her, pushing powerfully inside her body with a driving, relentless rhythm. And though her mind almost refused to accept what was happening to her, her body responded, answered his, moved against him.

She couldn't fight it, couldn't fight him. She bit her lip against the words that almost sprang to consciousness, for she was sure of one thing. He hadn't taken her by force. She hadn't exactly been a willing participant, but he hadn't forced himself upon her.

She'd never been with a man who was this clearly aroused, who was this relentless in finding his release. Yet in the midst of a need she sensed was almost painful in its intensity, he found the time to care for her. His hand moved between their joined bodies, he stroked her, she closed her eyes as her body began to respond and finally surrendered to his touch, to where he was taking her, to where he wanted her to go.

She climaxed again and felt his release, felt the quick, sharp pulsations directly following hers. Heard the low, anguished sound he made against her neck. And she surprised herself then, putting her arms tightly around his back, then up around his neck. She started to cry, but not because he'd hurt her in any way. She cried because she knew it was Chance, and knew he was the one man who could hurt her worse than any other person ever had in her life.

She felt scared and vulnerable as she lay in the large bed, his weight on top of her, considerable even though he rested his forearms on the mattress. He lifted his head, finally, and kissed her so tenderly that the sweetness of that simple gesture brought a fresh surge of tears to her eyes.

"Chance?" she said, and her voice shook with the effort.

His body stilled, and she knew that somehow, he knew she was different.

He rolled across the bed and turned on the bedside lamp. The room was bathed in a soft light; it was still dark outside. The world was sleeping, but as Cyn looked up into this man's face, she knew her own would never be the same.

Chapter Five

She looked heartbreakingly vulnerable sitting in the middle of the king-size bed, the sheets drawn up around her naked body. His back was to her, and he was careful to cover himself with some of those same sheets when he faced her.

Above all, he didn't want to scare her.

He knew she was struggling to find the right words, so he simply covered her hand with his own.

"Talk to me, Cyn."

"What happened?" Her voice broke on the last word, and she covered her face with her hands. Chance was ashamed of himself, taking advantage of her altered state in order to make sure she belonged to him.

"We're married."

"Oh, no!"

In answer, he got up, shrugged into his faded jeans, then strode over to the VCR and popped in the tape of the ceremony. Cyn watched, fascinated.

When it was over, he rewound the tape, ejected it and put it back in its case. Then he handed her the several photographs that had been included in their deluxe wedding package.

She looked at the photos, then at him, then at the photos, then at him.

He cleared his throat. She was his wife now, and deserved the best he had to offer her. Which included honesty.

"I don't know what happens to you, Cyn, but it's as if... you become someone different. I didn't want to lose you, or the baby, so I... took advantage of this last time when you were so willing to do whatever I wanted, and suggested that we get married."

"Can we get it annulled?"

"Nope. It's been consummated."

She glanced down at the bed and he watched her face as it heated.

"Do you remember?" He had to know.

She nodded her head, then tossed the photos on the bed.

He cleared his throat again against the sudden tightness. "I wanted you any way I could get you. You need someone to take care of you, Cyn, and I'm the man for the job. The ranch is pretty isolated, so I don't think you could get into that much trouble—"

She flew off the bed at him, and he found himself at the mercy of her pounding fists.

"You can't do this to me, I'm not going back to your ranch with you, I've been fine by myself all these years, and I'll be fine once you're gone—"

"No, you haven't, and no, you won't be." He was amazed at how calm he remained, holding her at bay, understanding her fury, her anger and frustration, at not being able to understand what had happened to her. "And I haven't been all that fine, either, Cyn."

That stopped her. She looked up at him, confused, and he remembered the expression she'd had on her face when they'd ridden the elevator up to their suite.

"You haven't?" she whispered.

"I've been lonely often enough to understand what loneliness can do to someone. And I've been alive long enough to realize that the world can work in some pretty strange ways. We're together for a reason, Cyn. Think about it. What are the odds of everything happening exactly the way it did?"

She was silent for a moment, then nodded her head. When she glanced back up at him, he was shocked at how tired she appeared.

"What should we do?"

She was looking at him for guidance, and he knew it. He couldn't fail her now.

"We have to talk to your sister."

"Oh, my God. Pepper. The baby." She couldn't imagine how her sister was going to take the news of her pregnancy when she herself had been trying so hard for so long.

"You'll have to tell her you'll be going back to the ranch with me."

She nodded her head.

"Forever, Cyn. Not just until the baby's born. None of that for us."

He could tell she was struggling with this. Her wedding vows, her commitment, hadn't been made at that little Vegas chapel, but would be made right now, here in this rumpled hotel bed.

He waited.

She glanced away from him. Chewed her lip. Tears filled her eyes.

He felt like every sort of bastard in the world, but he had to be tough, almost cruel, on this issue. They had to commit to each other, one hundred percent. She wasn't capable of being strong at this time, so he had to be strong for her. He had to protect her, and their baby, and the only way he could do that was if she came back to the ranch.

She nodded her head, and he knew he had her, but the knowledge didn't bring much joy with it. He wanted her to come to him of her own will, not because her hand had been forced.

But he'd take her any way he could.

"Let's get dressed and order up some breakfast. Then we'll go to your sister's."

A HOT SHOWER semirevived her spirits. As she dressed in the only clothes she had, her bridal mini and the exquisite underwear, Cyn wondered how she was ever going to make a life with this man.

He was kind. And good. She sensed she didn't have to be scared of him. But he was stronger than she was, and that was a disquieting discovery. She was used to being the strong one, first with her mother and then with her twin. She'd always been the one to make difficult decisions and act on them, the one others turned to when the job had to get done.

It felt so strange to lean on someone else.

She heard room service arrive, ran her fingers through her freshly washed hair one more time, then sailed out into the main suite trying to project a confidence she in no way felt.

She'd make it through today if it killed her.

SHE WAS SO MAGNIFICENT she took his breath away.

He'd ordered just about everything on the menu, not knowing what she liked, how she took her coffee or whether she preferred juice, how she liked her eggs, or if she even ate breakfast. He watched as she ate a few pieces of dry toast, then drank half a glass of orange juice.

And he remembered how Mark's wife had suffered from morning sickness.

"How's your stomach?" he asked.

She glanced up at him, then blushed.

"Fine. I haven't felt that sick—yet."

He nodded his head, then tucked into his bacon, eggs and hash browns. Living on the ranch, getting up before sunrise to start work, he always began the day with a large breakfast. He watched her as she picked up a piece of bacon, took a small bite, then set it down.

"How soon can you be ready to go?" he asked.

She took her time answering his question, and he was glad of that, as it showed him she was taking their arrangement seriously.

"Two days?"

"Fine."

"Should I sell the town house, or do you think we should keep it?"

"It's yours, you do whatever you want with it."

She nodded her head and took another bite of toast.

There was a tiny, exquisite bouquet of miniature pink roses on the tray, all part of the hotel's honeymoon special. Chance watched as Cyn glanced at the flowers, then her eyes filled with tears and she lowered her head so he wouldn't see.

Some wedding, he thought with a growing sense of frustration. And though he wasn't a self-pitying man by nature, he wondered at the peculiarities of life, and how they'd met. He wondered what would've happened if they'd met at another time, another place, had a more normal courtship, married in a more traditional way.

There was no point in thinking about it. One thing he'd learned when he was barely a boy was that life rarely gave you second chances. Or even good ones. You had to play the hand you'd been dealt.

THEY ARRIVED at Pepper's house a little before noon.

It was Luca's day off, and they were both out by the pool. Cyn watched her sister's expression as she took in Chance, and she could tell her twin was impressed.

Chance was also obviously on his best behavior now that he was meeting her family.

Introductions had barely been made, and Luca had just brought out a round of drinks, when Cyn decided to jump in with both feet.

"We got married yesterday."

Pepper choked on her drink, then stared at them both incredulously. Before she could stop herself, she blurted out, "But you never even mentioned his name to me!"

"I didn't give her much of a chance," Chance said with a smile. Cyn started as he took her hand and drew her to his side. "It was a pretty persistent courtship."

"I guess so!" Pepper said, her green eyes shining with happiness. "I never thought I'd see my sister married, and I'm so happy to meet the man who finally changed her mind!"

"There's one more thing," Cyn said around the tightness in her throat. She didn't want to hurt her sister, but she couldn't deceive her, either.

"Yes?" Luca said, his arm around his wife. They were both smiling delightedly, and Cyn gave them a long look, wanting to remember them this way. Happy.

She tried to get the words out. Couldn't. She looked up at Chance—her husband, what a strange thought— and knew her silent appeal was in her eyes.

Chance tightened his fingers around hers, and she drew a funny kind of strength from his presence.

"Cyn is pregnant. We're going to have a baby right around Christmas."

Cyn had been watching her twin, and now she saw Pepper's smile freeze into place. She was so brave, but Cyn could sense her anguish right beneath the surface.

"Oh, Cyn!" She threw herself into Cyn's arms, and hugged her fiercely. Then she started to cry.

Luca, a complex emotional expression on his face, started toward his wife. He put his hands on her shoulders, murmured something in Italian, then walked her into the house. Pepper behaved as if she were in a daze.

Cyn watched them go, then turned to Chance.

"This is going to be difficult for her."

"It's difficult for you."

"I can get through this. She's not as strong."

She heard the doorbell ring, and went to answer it. Deva stood at the door, a huge bowl of fruit salad in her hands.

"Cyn?" she said cautiously, and Cyn knew she'd picked up the emotional vibration of the day.

"Pepper's upstairs." She thought about what she was going to say, then decided to just come out with it. "I got married last night, and—I'm pregnant."

Deva's eyes widened, but she said nothing.

"The reason I'm telling you this is that she needs someone, and I don't think it's me."

Blessedly, Deva understood immediately and took charge.

"Here." She handed Cyn the fruit salad and headed toward the stairs.

Cyn felt as if she were on automatic pilot. She glanced back toward the sliding glass doors leading toward the patio area and saw Chance leaning in the doorway, watching her. She gave him a halfhearted smile, then went into the kitchen and put the salad in the refrigerator.

She stood there, wondering what she was going to say or do to make her twin's world all right again, when she felt large, warm, comforting hands on her shoulders.

"There's nothing you can do, Cyn. You can't fix this one."

She needed the comfort he was offering, and covered his hands with her own.

"I feel so... cruel. She's wanted a baby for so long, and I didn't even want to get pregnant." Cyn realized how her words had to sound to him, and she amended them. "What I mean is, I have nothing against getting pregnant, in fact, I never really thought it would happen for me, but—"

"I know what you mean." He rubbed her shoulders briefly, then let her go. "What do you want to do?"

She turned to face him. "I don't know if she wants to see me."

"Do you want to try?"

"This has to be very hard for her."

"How're you doing?"

She smiled up at him. He always watched out for her. It was a new feeling, and still disconcerting. But he was her husband now, and she had to get used to it.

In the past, she would have said that everything was fine, she was fine, no matter what she felt inside. But she had the most uncanny feeling that this man would see right through her to the lie, would see through any facade.

"Kind of shaky. Chance, she's like my other half. A part of me. We've always been together."

"How did you feel when she married Luca?"

"Happy for her." She looked up at him and those blue eyes were too clear, they saw too much. "But scared, too, because I thought it would never happen for me."

"She probably feels the same way."

She took his hand. It had to be hormones making her crazy, but she needed to lean on him. Let him make the decisions for a while. "What would you do?"

"I'd go home and give her some time. We won't leave for the ranch until you talk to her."

She studied his face and was suddenly thankful he'd been sent into her life, no matter how complicated things were bound to get. "Thank you."

They left quietly and went back to her town house.

THEY WERE EATING take-out Chinese when the doorbell rang. Cyn answered it and found Deva on her doorstep. The delicate blonde looked flustered.

"How is she?"

Deva sighed. "She's taking it pretty badly. It's not about you, Cyn, it's about her own failure to conceive."

"I know. Have you eaten, do you want some Chinese food?"

Deva shook her head. "No, I'm on my way to a class in self-hypnosis—"

Cyn didn't hear the rest because the blood began to pound in her ears.

Hypnosis.

Her strange behavior.

The blackouts.

Madame Babala.

Would you like me to give you a suggestion so that you will not pick up any of the hypnosis meant for your sister?

Oh, my God.

What was the word? The trigger? The nickname? Why hadn't she been paying attention and why had she thought the woman was a total fraud? She grabbed Deva's flowing, tie-dyed sleeve as the woman turned to go.

"Deva! Where was Madame Babala located?"

"Oh, are you thinking of taking one of her classes on past lives?"

Yeah, the one I had before her hypnotic suggestion.

"Ah—sort of."

Briefly, Deva gave her directions. Cyn thanked her, then shut the door and headed toward her husband.

"SO THIS WOMAN hypnotized your sister and it didn't take, but it did with you?"

"That's about the size of it."

"Can she undo it?"

"She'd better."

Cyn hadn't called for an appointment. She figured she'd storm right in and demand that Madame Babala undo whatever damage she'd done. Not the pregnancy, of course, but at least she'd stop having these weird episodes she couldn't remember.

At least there wasn't anything wrong with her. Oh, there was a lot that was wrong, but she could get this fixed and put an end to her erratic behavior.

Chance stopped his pickup truck at another red light. "Let me get this straight. There's a key word, and whenever a man says it, you become this warm, willing, insatiable sex machine who can't think of anything but sexual intercourse and impregnation?"

"Yep."

"I'm sure Madame Babala has her bad points, as well."

She slanted him a look and saw that he was grinning, and suddenly she saw the absurdity of the entire situation and began to laugh. He reached over and took her hand, and at that moment her future looked a whole lot brighter.

She could learn to love Chance. Maybe. Maybe he would even come to love her. If anyone was going to be able to blast through her years and years of defenses, it was this cowboy right beside her.

"MADAME IS NOT IN."

"What do you mean, not in!" Cyn could feel her composure starting to fray. The man who had answered the door looked like Bela Lugosi in *Plan 9 from Outer Space*, and had the accent to match. She guessed he was Madame Babala's butler, or houseman, or something.

"Madame will be returning from Hungary in three days. She will be glad to call you when she arrives home."

"Three days! But I can't wait that long."

"I'm sorry, I have no way of reaching her. She is at the family estate in the country, and there is no phone." He glowered at her from beneath bushy eyebrows. "You will have to come back."

"Can I have the very first appointment? It's an emergency."

"Of course. I will check her appointment book and rearrange her schedule myself. Give me your phone number and I will call you."

She did, then the massive door shut with a clang. Staring at it, Cyn saw the vampire's head doorknocker and wondered if the family estate wasn't really a family tomb.

Great. I'm starring in a Stephen King novel.

Chance stood by her side, and she looked up at him in utter defeat.

"We're screwed."

He put his arm around her as they headed back toward his truck. "Short of flying to Hungary, there's nothing we can do. I'll just have to keep a close eye on you for three days, and then we'll come back.''

''If I could only figure out what triggers it—''

''Whoa! No! Don't even think about the word—''

''But I don't know what it is. I think I was so embarrassed learning about Pepper and Luca's sex life that—''

''She told Madame Babala about her sex life?'' He was stunned.

''Well…yeah. I mean, she wanted a baby.…'' When he didn't answer while thinking this one over, she went on. ''Okay, so it was some little nickname he gave her—''

''When did she give you two this suggestion?'' Chance asked.

She narrowed her eyes. ''What are you getting at?''

''Is there a chance the baby might be someone else's?''

She twisted away from him, but he held fast. ''Oh, I knew it! I knew you were too good to be true, that you'd look for a way to get out of this! Forget it, you've got your annulment, and—''

''Will you listen to me a minute? I want to make sure that some schmuck out here doesn't go running off without a clue that he's about to become a father—''

She stopped struggling against him and relaxed. ''Okay. Fair enough. I went with Pepper to this Madame Babala—'' Chance opened the truck door for her and she slid inside. ''Thank you.'' He shut the door, then she unlocked the driver's side door and waited for him to climb in before she continued her story.

"—So she asked me if I wanted some sort of—suggestion, so I wouldn't pick up on the hypnosis."

"And you didn't take it?"

"No, I didn't even believe that the whole thing worked if you want to know the truth. I thought she was a big fat fraud. And then that same day, that evening, I went to The Branding Iron and met you."

He smiled, and she gave him a quick dig in the ribs. He grabbed her hand, then held it as he maneuvered the truck through traffic.

"Okay, Cyn, here's the plan. We lay low for three days until this Madame Babala returns, then she undoes the suggestion, and then we go back to the ranch."

"Chance," she said slowly, fighting not to let her fear get in the way. "If there wasn't a baby on the way, would you—"

"Yes."

"What I mean is—"

"Yes."

"No, wait a minute, listen to what I—"

"Yes." He still had ahold of her hand, and he brought her fingers to his lips and kissed them. "I wanted you from the first moment I saw you. Yes, yes, yes."

THEY WENT OUT to a barbecue place and had ribs, then came home and watched television. Chance wasn't quite sure what Cyn would want to do about sleeping arrangements that evening. After all, they were married, and he wanted to start acting like a real married couple as soon as possible. But, as she so blithely informed him after dinner, "We still haven't had sex together."

"What do you mean?" he said. "What were we doing this morning? That was you there, wasn't it?" It was still disconcerting to realize he'd been making love to a woman under the influence—of hypnosis.

"Well it was, but not when it started."

Now he was totally confused. "Where were you?"

"I was—dreaming."

"What?"

"I was dreaming. I thought—I thought I was having a sex dream. You know what I mean, don't you?"

Do I ever. He'd been having nothing but sexual dreams during the few naps he'd taken after meeting her. Cowboys didn't normally take naps, and he was no exception. But when he and Cyn had been in bed together the last few nights, they hadn't exactly been sleeping.

She was a charming, but exhausting, companion.

Now he knew she was embarrassed to be talking about this, because her pale complexion flushed a fiery red.

"It's okay, Cyn. You can tell me anything."

"You started making love to me, and by the time— oh, God, this is too embarrassing—"

"Tell me."

"By the time I woke up, you were already inside me. I couldn't stop it—"

He felt lower than a snake. "You mean...did I...did you think I was—"

"No. No! I was really enjoying myself, and I'd be a hypocrite to say anything else. But I—I feel kind of self-conscious with you about sex."

"Why?" He couldn't fathom why. They'd done just about everything a man and woman could do together, without any shame or inhibitions. She had a lusty sensuality that knocked his socks off. He loved her for it.

"Because when we really do have sex . . . without the hypnosis thing—it might not be any good—"

"Not a chance."

"How can you be so sure?"

"Because the way you turn me on, it'll never be bad for the rest of our lives. I don't care if it's a quickie before I head out to the barn or a long, slow night of lovemaking in the winter, it's never going to be bad between us." He stopped talking long enough to be stunned by this considerable revelation. She was something, his wife. He'd talked more with her in the past few days than he had with most of the hired hands for months at a time.

Hell, she was a lot like his horse. He talked to his pinto gelding, Pancho, a lot while he was out riding the fence line. But he restrained himself from telling Cyn this, knowing she wouldn't understand and probably wouldn't appreciate being compared to a horse.

"But it was you having sex—making love—with me this morning," he insisted. He was going to give it his best shot, and attempt to spend the night in her bed.

"The first part—when I was half asleep—I think I was still under the influence of Madame Babala."

"So what you're saying," Chance said slowly, trying to understand what she was getting at, "is that you're scared you're going to be a lousy lay once the hypnotic suggestion is reversed."

"I might not have chosen to use those particularly blunt, crude, masculine words, but yes, that's the general gist of it."

He started to laugh, and pulled her into his arms. "Not a chance, honey. Not a chance."

"But what if I can't—keep up?"

"I'll wait for you."

"What if I'm not as responsive—"

"You will be."

"What if—"

"Don't worry," he whispered, just before he kissed her. "I'm a very patient man."

"WE HAVE TO DISCUSS one last thing," he said as he started down the stairs from her linen closet to the couch, his arms piled high with blankets, sheets and several pillows.

"What?"

"What happens if somehow, and I mean by accident, you get triggered?"

"You mean if one of us says—the word."

"Yeah."

She smiled down at him from the upper stairs. "Ah, just go ahead and enjoy yourself. Live it up. Make me happy. Whip me, beat me, make me write bad checks."

He was so grateful he had numerous blankets concealing him so she couldn't see what her words were doing to his body.

SHE POPPED SOME microwave popcorn, and they watched a late night movie snuggled up on the couch. She let him kiss her, but he knew he wasn't going to get much further.

"I hope you don't think I'm some sort of tease," she whispered as they both came up for air. "It's just that—the next time we really get down to it, I'd like to be me and not some hypnotically crazed woman in heat."

He simply nodded his head, not trusting his voice. One thing he'd discovered long ago was that men and women looked at sex in completely different ways.

Men were much less discriminating.

She stood up and stretched, announcing she was about to go to bed while he tried to ignore her curvy little body and intently channel-surfed with the remote control. He came to an abrupt halt when he saw Luca, a chef's hat on his head, stirring something in a saucepan.

"Hey, it's your brother-in-law!"

"Wow!" She sat back down on the couch and started to laugh. "He did about seven or eight of these shows, just guest spots, but they drove him crazy. Luca likes to be in control, and in his kitchen, he is. It's a whole other story in a television studio, though.''

''Now, you've marinated the chicken livers in white wine, and after they've been gently sautéed in the butter sauce, you can add various spices—''

Cyn stood up and stretched, then yawned. ''You'll enjoy this one. I'll see you tomorrow, Chance—''

''—Salt, thyme, even a little cayenne pepper—''

He was watching her stretch, not the show, and he almost went into complete cardiac arrest as she flipped her T-shirt over her head, then unhooked the front fastening of her black lace bra.

''Cyn?'' he said. ''Are you sure—''

She'd already slipped off her shorts and panties, and snuggled beneath the afghan next to him. Taking his face in her hands, she gave him such a blatantly sexual kiss that, when he finally surfaced for air, he expected to see smoke coming out of his ears.

''Cyn, I—''

She already had her hands in his pants.

''Ah, I—oh boy—um, if you could stop just for a minute. . . .''

She did, looking up at him with such a devilish expression on her face that his toes curled inside his boots. They were in for a long, wild night.

''Yes?''

He thought back to their conversation on the stairway.

Enjoy yourself. Live it up. Make me happy.

He'd certainly try.

"Nothing." He stood up and took off his boots, then unfastened his jeans. She was already at work on his shirt, and buttons were flying.

Hell, it was a dirty job. But someone had to do it.

Chapter Six

Chance woke up the following morning with Cyn snuggled up against him. They were, fittingly enough, back in her bed where it had all started, nestled between the jungle-print sheets. Judging from the light outside the bedroom window, it was just a little after sunrise.

Every muscle in his body ached, and he was a cowboy who was accustomed to heavy work. He stretched, then grimaced as certain muscles pulled. Glancing over at Cyn, he smiled as he saw the wild cloud of dark red hair spread across the leopard-print pillow. She was sleeping soundly, breathing deeply, and he knew he would let her sleep as late as she wanted.

He reached over to the bedside phone and turned off the bell. Then he slid back beneath the covers and thought about how to get this entire escapade under control. He liked being in control, it was one of the things in his life he did rather well. He prided himself on it, in fact. After Annie, and what had happened to their marriage, he'd been determined never to let him-

self get out of control again. It was just too dangerous.

Yet he'd been out of control, on a certain level, ever
since he'd met Cyn. Things had escalated rapidly, and
if he'd sat back for one moment and let common sense
guide any of his actions, he probably wouldn't be lying here in this bed with her. He would've headed back
to the ranch, running for his life, away from women,
and commitment, and the heartache that one word always seemed to imply.

But if he was honest with himself, and looked at his
life unflinchingly, in the last few years of his life common sense hadn't brought him much in the way of fulfillment. Common sense and doing the right thing, the
correct thing, had brought him a lot of loneliness. Hell,
the closest thing he'd had to a relationship had been his
horse, Pancho. He stretched out in bed, his hands behind his head as he grinned. That would make an interesting "Oprah." The women in the audience would
have a field day analyzing a man who could only commit to his horse.

They had two days to go before Madame Babala
came back, two days in which to get to know each
other better. He didn't want to trigger Cyn again. He
wanted the next time they made love to be a deepening
of the bond they shared. Right now, the deepest bond
they had was the baby they had created. He wanted
more.

He slid over beside her in the queen-size bed and put
his arms around her. He hadn't felt such a longing to

protect a woman for some time. Cyn, as prickly and temperamental as she was, brought that longing out in him. And it was more than the fact that she was pregnant.

Chance had always believed, from the time he was a small child, that things happened for a reason. While his mother had still been alive, she'd attempted to instill a certain amount of spiritual thought into her only son. It had taken deep root, and as he lay in bed he knew that his entire meeting with Cyn, the way they'd connected, her utter surrender under the hypnotic suggestion, all of it had been meant to happen.

He understood her in the way that one caretaker understood another. Sometimes you were thrust into that role by fate, sometimes you used it so you didn't have to take too close a look at your own life. He'd had it both ways, but lately had felt so very empty, so lonely, as if life was utterly devoid of any meaning. That had been when he'd decided to come to Las Vegas and kick up his heels.

In retrospect, he wasn't totally proud of his intentions. He'd wanted to get laid. Hot sex with no strings. But what he'd really been after, in his heart of hearts, had been some sort of connection with another human being that went beyond the superficialities of day-to-day existence.

He'd wanted to feel that he wasn't alone.

What were the odds that after Madame Babala had been through with Cyn that she should just happen to walk into The Branding Iron and he should see her?

He'd been aware of her the moment she'd walked in that door. He'd wanted her with an intensity that had shaken him to his core.

What had really scared him was that, for one brief moment as she'd stood poised in that doorway, he'd wanted her more than he even wanted his ranch.

The C & M Ranch was more than a workplace to him. There was something about the land that gave him strength. Originally, he'd wanted to work his father's land, turn it into a place his children would be proud of, so he could look back on all his hard work at the end of his life with quiet satisfaction. Instead, his father had loved the bottle more than any land, had mismanaged things badly.

Chance had struggled to right things, to fix things, but he hadn't succeeded. He'd still been a teenager when they'd lost the ranch, his family's land, and he hadn't been able to get it back. One of the most painful things in his life had been the moment he'd realized he was simply going to have to walk away.

He'd started over. Built up from nothing. Met and married Annie—and lost all over again.

But there had to be something to that expression that the third time is always the charm. This time, he'd gone into business with his favorite cousin, Mark. They'd worked long hours and made conservative, business-like decisions. He simply hadn't had a life for years at a time, except for working the ranch. And he'd had a vision, a dream, that the C & M Ranch was going to be known around the world for its prize-winning cattle.

And now he was bringing another woman back into the whole equation.

He should have been scared. He wasn't. As a rancher, one of the skills he valued most was instinct. Something could fly in the face of his best guess, but if it felt wrong, it had always been his experience that he eventually lived to regret it.

He didn't regret meeting Cyn. She'd been the perfectly designed package of feminine emotional dynamite needed to wake him up out of his deep freeze. Oh, he was well aware of how he came across to others. Solid. Dependable. Perhaps even a little dull. What would surprise anyone was that deep inside that placid exterior beat the heart of a total romantic, a man who felt things deeply.

You couldn't decide to be a rancher in this day and age without some of that feeling. Even attempting to make a profit, to break even in the face of overwhelming odds that you wouldn't, necessitated that you had some emotional investment. He couldn't feel halfway about the land in the same way that he couldn't feel halfway about Cyn. He hadn't been able to go into a relationship with her in a semicommitted or casual manner. It had to be all or nothing.

He still wasn't proud of the way he'd coerced her into marriage, but he took his responsibilities seriously. He couldn't protect her, and their unborn child, if she wasn't with him. In the short time—hell, in the *days* he'd known Cyn, and it had still been less than a week—he knew she had just as deep a sense of commitment as he did. That would surely help them make a go of this unusual marriage.

He slid even closer to her, wanting to feel her skin against his. Not sex, not lovemaking, just simple closeness. He loved the scent of her hair against his face, the soft coolness of her body against his, the way her skin could flush with heat and transfer that sensual burn to him. He loved just about everything about her. As he drifted off to sleep again, Chance thought that finding this woman in his arms more than made up for any of the hardships he'd met up with in life.

SHE DRIFTED AWAKE in his arms, and for one terrible moment felt totally out of control.

He was breathing deeply, his face turned into her hair, his arms entwined around her. His skin touched hers the length of their bodies beneath the coolness of the sheets, and she derived a certain comfort from that sensation.

She trusted him to take care of her, and that in itself was nothing short of astounding.

She knew how she sometimes came off to others. Bossy. Demanding. Impossibly high standards. What no one had ever understood was how lonely it was being the one in charge. No one in her family would have ever known from the facade she presented to the world at large, but there had been many times when she'd been terrified making all the decisions. She only had to close her eyes to see her mother's gentle, confused expression, or Pepper's frightened face. She didn't know how or why, but from the time she could remember, they'd both always turned to her.

Her mother had died when she and Pepper had been in their twenties, and she couldn't even remember most of the dreams she'd had. She'd only known that she had to find a way to support them both, they had to survive. She'd worked at a bank at the time, and a friend had just taken a test and gotten her real estate license. Cyn borrowed her books, took an extension course at the local university, and got hers as well.

She'd never looked back.

She'd done astoundingly well because she'd inspired confidence in her clients. She knew what a home really represented because she'd never had one. Year after year, she'd outsold the competition. In the upstairs closet off the guest bedroom there were boxes containing her awards and certificates. She'd never unpacked them, and now, lying in bed, she wondered why.

They hadn't truly meant anything to her. Selling real estate had simply been a means to an end, enabling Pepper to take the series of gourmet cooking classes that were to enable her to work in the hotel industry. But then she had met Luca, married him, and the direction of her dreams had changed. Cyn had felt that her sister didn't need her anymore, and she hadn't known what to do with herself.

It had been so hard to simply stop.

Then Pepper had wanted to have a baby, and she'd taken over again, but this time it had led her life in a direction that she couldn't have predicted....

For the first time in her life, she was going to be in a position where she had to think about what she wanted. She had to take care of herself because she was going to have a child.

No, you have to take care of yourself because it's past time....

She knew she had to put some distance between herself and her twin, but it had hurt to see Pepper in pain over her pregnancy. Everything had happened so suddenly, it was as if decisions were being made for her.

She closed her eyes and shared her thoughts in her own peculiar type of prayer.

I asked you for a sign, but I really meant it for Pepper. But perhaps you meant it for me. A sign. A man. A direction for my life. A child. I'm not sure if I'm up to this, but what else is new? I want to be up for this, I don't want to let Chance down. On one level, I think he deserves better than a goofball like me, but then who am I to judge what he wants or should have? Just please, if I can ask for one little thing. Please don't let him regret his decision, this marriage, or taking me back to his ranch.

She opened her eyes, then moved slightly to let Chance know she was in the process of waking up.

HE'D BEEN THINKING for a long time, and he had an answer.

"I think I know what might have triggered you," he whispered as she turned from her side to her back and looked up at him.

"Should I be embarrassed?" she said, and he found that he liked the way she looked in the morning. Some women woke up trashed, just total wrecks. Cyn looked fresh and sweet. There was still this little touch of innocence to her, and he found it quite a turn-on.

"Nope. Not with me."

"How did you figure out the word?"

"It had to be something in that recipe last night, and my guess would be that it would have to be an ingredient that would have a double meaning for Pepper and Luca. Or an action. Like whisk. I don't think it's the word *whisk,* but if there was some secret meaning that the word held for the two of them—"

"Why are you figuring this out?"

"So we won't have a repeat of last night."

"I kind of figured out that something had happened when I woke up last night and you were in bed with me."

"I just took you at your word."

She seemed a little nervous. "Did you make me write bad checks?"

He laughed. He was definitely nervous, though he tried to project a controlled front. "Are you angry?"

"No." She smiled up at him, slowly, and he found his heart felt as if it were turning over. "No, I feel relaxed and happy and...complete."

"Good. Anyway, I thought that I might take you through a few of the words and try to hit on the right one. Then, once we understand the trigger, we can relax for the next forty-eight hours until we contact Madame Babala.''

''Okay.''

He liked the way she immediately trusted him to make plans for both of them. It was a quality that Annie had never quite been able to master. Now he put his arm around her and drew her head to his shoulder.

''This shouldn't be too painful,'' he teased.

''Just get on with it.'' Her playful tone belied the message in her words.

''All right. Chicken.''

''Nope.''

''Liver?''

''Uh-uh.''

''Sauté.''

''No.''

''Butter.''

''Last Tango in Paris.''

''This isn't a word-association game.''

''The hell it's not.'' She leaned over and gave him a quick, playful kiss, and he thought about discontinuing this particular game and beginning another.

''Wine?''

''Nah.''

''Spices.''

She shook her head.

''Salt—''

''—Of the earth.'' She laughed, and he hugged her tightly against him.

''Thyme.''

"We have all the thyme in the world—"

"You're not into puns, are you?"

"I like a good one now and then."

"Cookie is going to try and steal you away."

"Is he cute?"

He pinched her bottom and she yelped.

"He's almost seventy-five."

"Older men can be quite stimulating."

"Brat."

"Tease."

"Okay, let's get back to work. Marinate."

"I get shudders thinking about their sex life if that was the special word."

He threw back his head and laughed. "Like making love in a tub full of Jell-O."

She started to laugh, and it was a few minutes before they both settled down.

"Okay. I'll try just a few more, and then I'll give it up and just resign myself to baby-sitting you until we see the Madame. Pepper."

"That would be clever, that's her name. Nope."

He sighed. Funny, he'd been sure that he would be able to get to the bottom of things, find the key word, and at last have some modicum of control until the hypnotic suggestion was reversed.

They couldn't keep going on like this. He was a strong man and had more than his share of masculine stamina, but all this sex taking him by surprise was going to be the death of him.

He had to get things back under control.

Chance pictured the television show in his mind's eye: Luca in his chef's hat, gently stirring the chicken livers in the pan, adding the various spices, talking animatedly to the audience—

"Cayenne." The minute he thought the word, the second he said it, he knew he'd hit the jackpot.

She didn't say a word, simply slid on top of him and started to kiss him, using a lot of tongue action.

Bingo.

"Honey," he said, breaking off between kisses to get some air, "you can't overexert yourself, you've got to rest, I want you to rest—"

She covered his mouth with hers, and his traitorous body reacted as if it had a will of its own. His mind might have said no, but his body was made for yes.

Her skin, her scent, her breasts, her hair, her mouth, that mouth, moving lower, along his body, grazing over a nipple—

"Cyn," he panted, hating this weakness that seemed to be overtaking the logical, controlled center of his brain. "Cyn, I want you to rest, I *command* you to rest—"

"Your wish is my command, but we have to have sex first."

"No, I mean, right now—"

"—I know." She caught his mouth again.

He broke away. "No, I mean the second part of that sentence. Sleep, rest, no more activity."

"But we're lying down." Her voice sounded so innocent, while what she was doing to him as she moved lower on his body was most decidedly not.

"Cyn, I—oh, God . . ."

He surrendered.

THEY WOKE UP LATE in the afternoon, after a morning's romp that topped anything that had been done the night before. As Chance slowly came back to the land of the living, he thought that the top of his head had been blown off.

And he didn't even care.

When he glanced at her, he could immediately sense her mood. She was sitting in a chair facing the bed, wrapped in a knee-length, pink terry-cloth robe. On any other redhead, it would have clashed terribly, but somehow, on Cyn, it looked terrific.

"What's wrong?" He decided to jump right in. Hell, it took a smart man to admit he just didn't understand women worth beans.

"Aren't you going to miss me?"

"Miss you? Where are you going?"

"I mean, after I'm fixed."

His first thought was of the annual springtime cattle castrating on the ranch, and he shook his head to clear it.

"Fixed? You mean Madame Babala?"

She nodded her head.

"Cyn, we've been through this before. Now, come on, honey, you know you're safe with me."

"Won't you even miss her a little bit?"

He carefully considered how to word his reply, knowing that success depended on finding the exact, correct words and not stalling too long.

"I'll treasure the memories, but I won't miss—her." God, this was weird.

"I don't know that my—true sexual personality is that wild."

"You'll be just fine."

"You must have found the triggering word."

"I sure did—and we won't use it again."

They were silent for a few seconds, then Cyn blurted out, "Would you like to use the shower first?"

He mustered the most hopeful expression that he could. "I was kind of hoping we might take one together."

She looked so shy, he let her off the hook.

"That's okay. You go first."

She surprised him then, getting up, crossing to the bed and giving him a kiss that rivaled anything Miss Cayenne had given him in the last few days.

"That," she whispered, "is for being such a good man. A nice—"

He covered her lips with his, kissed her back, then whispered, "Don't say it. It's the kiss of death to a man's ego to hear that word."

She laughed, then glanced down to where her terry-cloth robe had come undone. He followed her gaze, and saw the soft shadow of her cleavage, the upper curve of her full breasts. His throat tightened, and he cleared it.

"I might take that shower first, after all." He glanced around the room for his clothing, then remembered they'd both torn it off him downstairs.

"Could I trouble you for a towel?" He didn't want her to see his obvious arousal.

She was grinning as she left the room, and he decided there was nothing much left to hide, after all.

AFTER THEIR SHOWERS, after lunch, they decided to laze away an afternoon shopping and sightseeing.

"How dangerous can it be?" Chance asked her as they went to the local mall. "We just have to stay away from cookware stores, markets and Mexican restaurants."

As Cyn still didn't know the trigger, she merely gave him one of those feminine, inscrutable looks he could never figure out.

They walked and laughed, took in a movie, bought ice cream cones, and generally made a day of it. And Chance thought, later that evening, that he hadn't had a day like the one they'd shared in a long time. He wondered if she would like life on the ranch, or if it would grow as tediously punishing for her as it had seemed to Annie.

He didn't want to compare the two women, but he knew that women suffered in isolation much more than men did. He could ride the fence line for days, or spend weeks at a time at the line camp, fifty miles from the main ranch. He loved his solitude, especially when he was close to nature. But women, they were different. Much more sociable.

He wondered how he could bring up the subject with her without making her feel that he had no faith in her ability to enjoy ranch life.

"Chance?"

He looked up and saw her standing in front of the fireplace. He thought she looked cute, in jeans and a kelly green sweatshirt. She'd been packing for part of the evening, figuring out what she would need to take to the ranch. They'd decided she would mail most of her stuff, whatever she didn't need right away, and take just the necessities with her. She'd already decided to sublet her town house to Deva until she could figure out what she was going to do with it.

"Yeah?"

"I'm going to bed now."

"Okay." He paused, not quite sure how to handle this, or what to say. "I'll probably stay up a little longer."

"Okay. See you in the morning."

He nodded his head. She went up the stairs, and he knew she needed the time, just a little time away from him. He'd blown into her life with the force of a tornado, not letting up until they'd stood in front of that Elvis fellow and said their vows in front of God and man.

She had a right to a few nights of privacy. Every bride did. And even if most of their wedding had been slightly off kilter and out of order, he didn't mind letting her have some time alone. God knows, she'd have plenty of time at the ranch.

He kicked off his boots and stretched out full length on the couch by the fire. Chance thought about the two of them sleeping in separate bedrooms. He frowned.

All that will change when I get her back to the ranch. There, he was king. It was his domain. She would sleep in his bedroom, in his bed, right next to him, in his arms, every single night of their lives.

She would belong to him, and they could start their marriage for real.

THEY SAW MADAME BABALA the minute she got into town.

When Cyn had referred to her as a "big fat fraud," Chance had assumed she had a figure that resembled a sumo wrestler's. He was surprised to find that this Madame had a stunning figure, high cheekbones, dark hair and eyes, and a very knowing gaze.

He was further surprised to find that he liked her immediately and without reservation.

She took no blame for what had happened to Cyn, and simply said that it was what life had in store for her. She asked Cyn if she was happy, and Chance was glad to hear her answer yes. Then she took Cyn into a back office to remove the hypnotic suggestion.

But first, they had a brief conversation outside that back office's door.

"You're sure you don't want me to ask her to plant a little suggestion that might make things—easier."

"Nope." He was gazing around Madame Babala's immense house. He'd never seen anything like it, except in the movies. Red velvet drapes let in barely any sunlight. The only room that saw the light of day was her spacious living room. The rest of the rooms seemed closed off. Shadowy.

Her furniture was all heavy, dark wood. Strange statues adorned shelves, bizarre sketches graced the walls. The effect was something between a deranged castle's decor and a museum designed by Tim Burton.

"I'd like to see this place on Halloween," Chance muttered. But he liked the decor as much as he liked her. He trusted her to put things right with Cyn.

"You're sure? I mean, like a hypnotic suggestion that might help me."

That caught his attention.

"Help you with what?"

"You know—being wild."

He didn't know how to answer that, for, in the bizarreness that was their relationship, he could honestly say that he still hadn't slept with his wife.

"What kind of help do you need?" he asked, and the minute he saw her face turn bright red, he knew.

"Can I ask you a question?" she whispered, her hands covering her face. She was that embarrassed.

"Yeah." He already knew what she was going to ask, and how he would have to answer.

"Did I—"

"Did you ever."

"Every time?"

"Like clockwork. Ba-boom."

She sighed. "That doesn't always happen to me."

He waited. She sighed again, then lowered her hands from her face.

"That's not entirely true. It never happens to me. Not that way." She lowered her voice to a whisper. "Not—without a lot of help."

Her total vulnerability touched him. Chance nodded his head, then took her hand. He knew how responsive and passionate she was in bed, but he couldn't take credit for it because it had had nothing to do with him.

"What about that time you woke up?" He wanted to look on the bright side. He wanted to think about getting their sex life back to normal, if either of them would ever be normal again.

"I started out really relaxed—"

"See? There you go. We'll get it, it might take a little time, but I'm willing to work hard—"

She punched his shoulder when she saw his grin, and he gave her a quick kiss on her cheek. This woman brought out the best in him. When he was with her, he felt witty, funny, incredibly confident. Then, with a look, a remark, a gesture, she could make him feel like he knew absolutely nothing about the opposite sex.

What a challenge. What a woman.

Madame Babala chose that moment to appear at the door to her office. "Are you ready, Cinnamon?"

She nodded, then stood up and walked toward the office.

"No more suggestions," Chance called after her, his voice gentle. "I just want you."

He was rewarded by her shaky grin right before the heavy wooden door closed behind her.

Chapter Seven

"Cayenne, huh?"

They were sitting at a local McDonald's, enjoying a fast meal after leaving Madame Babala's house. Cyn had listened intently as Chance reconstructed their entire relationship. A relationship that had hinged on sex and one particular word.

He stuck a fry into some ketchup, then popped it into his mouth. "Amazing how much trouble one little word can cause."

She felt comfortable with him, despite everything that had happened. She also found that she liked looking at him. He was handsome, in a rugged out-doorsy sort of way. She'd never had a particular thing for cowboys, but she liked this cowboy. If she'd had to pick a husband to spend the rest of her life with, she could've done a lot worse than Chance.

"So," he said now, after finishing off his Quarter Pounder, "when do you want to head back to the ranch?"

She sensed that he wanted to get back to work, back to the world he knew. She also had the feeling that he was proud of his ranch and wanted to show it to her. There were so many questions she wanted to ask him, chief among them being whether he was happy—really happy—about their coming baby.

Cyn sighed and took a sip of her Coke. She'd have plenty of time to ask him all the questions she wanted once they were living in Wyoming, out in the middle of nowhere. That is, if she had the nerve.

It scared her, this move out to the ranch. She wasn't exactly what one called a happy camper. She'd never been that athletic, and her idea of camping always included air-conditioning and room service. This match-up with Chance had been orchestrated entirely by fate, with a huge helping hand from Madame Babala. She wondered if, had she met him in any normal fashion, they would've dated for a while and then moved on.

The baby made that speculation impossible.

She sighed again, then glanced away from his knowing gaze. Well, people have started marriages with a whole lot less than what they had. The one thought that gave her the most comfort was the fact that Chance, at heart, seemed like a good man. She knew he would never physically hurt her. She wasn't so sure what effect he'd eventually have on her heart.

"I'd like to go to my doctor for a checkup—"

"Absolutely. I'll go with you."

She had to smile at how doggedly protective he was of her.

"Maybe he knows someone out in your area—"

"Eunice will know. I can call her tonight if that would make you feel better."

She already knew that Eunice was his cook and housekeeper, and that Cookie had been working on the ranch forever. When Chance and his cousin, Mark, had bought the place, they hadn't had the heart to ask him to leave.

"Yeah, it would." She swallowed against the sudden emotion that leapt into her throat. "And I'd like to try to talk with my sister."

Chance nodded his head. "We could go over there tonight."

Cyn stared at the food on the plastic tray between them. She hadn't eaten much; she didn't have any appetite. The several times she'd tried calling Pepper, Luca had told her she was asleep, or out, or not feeling well. The tone of his voice had told her he didn't enjoy lying for his wife.

Cyn knew her sister wasn't deliberately trying to be mean. It was just such a painful adjustment, to know that your sister was pregnant when you couldn't seem to conceive.

"I think I'd like that. I have to let her know I'm leaving, and she won't have a chance to see me for a while."

He surprised her then, reaching across the booth's table and taking her hand in his. "We'll figure out ways to get you back here. I don't want you to think you're going to be totally isolated out in the country."

She sensed a deeper fear behind his words, and wondered if there had been another woman who had voiced her displeasure concerning the C & M Ranch.

She squeezed his hand, more for her own reassurance than his. "I'm sure I'll be fine."

THEY ARRIVED AT HER sister's house just after dinner.

Luca met them at the door, assuring them he could quickly whip something up in the kitchen. Chance had to tell him they'd already had dinner almost three times before he was content to simply fix a pot of coffee and bring out some freshly baked chocolate *biscotti*.

"She's upstairs," he informed Cyn as he poured the coffee. The three of them were sitting in the living room, as Pepper had yet to put in an appearance.

"Do you think she'd mind if I went up?" Cyn asked. She hated this new sense of uncertainty she felt with her twin.

"I think you'd better. I don't see her coming down." Luca passed Chance the plate of *biscotti*.

"We'll be fine," Chance said, and she knew he was doing his best to reassure her. "It'll give Luca and I a chance to get acquainted."

She gave him a look that clearly said she didn't believe this male-bonding smokescreen for an instant. They were simply going to wait downstairs until she'd had a chance to try to talk to Pepper.

Nervous, she grabbed one of the bigger *biscotti* off the plate, then took a swallow of her coffee. She'd drowned it in milk, so it wasn't too hot. She took another sip, then set the cup down and, cookie in hand, headed toward the stairs.

"WOMEN," LUCA SAID, shaking his head. "I have no idea how they think, what they want, how they operate." He poured Chance another cup of coffee. "I would rather cook a dinner for five hundred and create three complicated ice sculptures than have one of those special conversations they want. Do you know what I mean?"

Chance nodded his head. He had to smile. Luca was clearly volatile, but had no chance of being the champion when either Cyn or her twin were in the room.

"They're something, aren't they?" he said.

"That they are."

"Do you have any in-laws?" Chance knew it was shameless of him, but he wanted to use these few moments he had with Luca to find out more about Cyn. She was intensely private when it came to her personal life.

"Hmm. I'm not surprised she didn't mention her mother to you. The woman was—unstable. Their father left before the twins were born. I cannot understand a man doing that."

Chance sipped his coffee and considered this. No wonder Cyn didn't trust easily. Nothing in her life thus far had led her to believe she could.

"She died before I met my wife. She has pictures, if you would like to see—"

"That's all right. I just wondered if Cyn had any more relatives living in the area."

"No. The sisters just have each other. They're very close."

Chance nodded, then glanced in the direction Cyn had taken. He hoped that, whatever happened this evening, the twins had an opportunity to patch things up.

"HEY," CYN SAID softly as she walked into the bedroom. Her twin was curled up in bed, staring out the window.

Pepper flushed, then sat up and smoothed her tangled hair back with her hands. "Luca didn't tell me you were here."

Cyn took a deep breath. "I don't think you would have seen me if he had."

Pepper looked down at her hands, clearly nervous.

Cyn bit her lip, trying to find the right words. She'd made Madame Babala promise never to reveal what had happened as a result of the hypnosis, and talked with Chance about the same thing. She couldn't bear it if her child were to hear about the circumstances of her conception as if they were a joke.

Chance had agreed with her instantly.

Now, for the first time in her life, she was going to keep a very necessary secret from her twin. Pepper had always known everything about her, but this was something that had to remain between only her and Chance.

She had no worries about Madame Babala. The woman was mysterious enough, one more secret would be a piece of cake.

She could, however, tell her twin just a little of the circumstances.

"Pep," she began, keeping her voice very soft. "Neither of us planned on this happening."

Her twin merely nodded her head, still unable to meet her eyes.

"I haven't even known Chance that long."

Pepper nodded again.

Well, at least she was listening. At least she wasn't in such an emotional state that she'd thrown her out of the bedroom. That had to count for something.

"When we found out I was pregnant—" She hurried over the word as if by making that simple gesture she could spare her sister any more pain. "When we found out, we decided that it would be—best if we got married."

"You mean, he did."

Cyn smiled. How well her sister knew her, and her fears.

"Yeah." She swallowed against her tight throat. "But I never meant to hurt you—"

"I know." Finally, ever so slowly, her twin met her gaze. "I know I'm being really selfish. But I hurt, Cyn. I hurt so much, I can't even begin to describe it to you. Every time I see a baby, every time there's a commercial on TV, or when I catch Luca staring out the window and I know what he's thinking. Cyn, he's one of *nine* children. He's wanted a baby from the start, he's always been honest about that. If I can't give him a child of his own, I'm going to have to leave him.''

''You can't do that!''

''I don't know what else to do.''

''We'll think of something—''

''No. You've looked after me long enough. It's time you concentrated on your own life. It's past time. I want you to start your marriage with no worries. I don't want to drag you down with my problems—''

''It was never like that—''

''It *was!* Don't you think I know? All my life, you've been the strong one and I've been the one who leaned on you. I wanted to lean on Mom, but that was impossible, so I just turned it all on you. And you're so damned...*competent*. Competent. I've wanted a baby for almost eighteen months and I can't get pregnant. You don't even particularly *want* to have children, you weren't even *looking* to get pregnant, and bingo, you're going to have a baby.''

It hurt, listening. More than Cyn wanted to admit. And as she listened, she realized her twin had paid a price for the roles they'd both been thrust into, so long ago.

Pepper seemed to have run out of steam, and now she simply sat in the middle of the king-size bed, looking like a lost little girl.

Cyn knew she had to, in a fashion, say goodbye.

''We're leaving for his ranch in the next few days.''

Pepper didn't say anything.

"I'm subletting the town house to Deva."

"She told me."

"Chance says we'll come back for visits. All the time." She cleared her throat, hoping her voice wouldn't change and reveal her precarious emotions. "Maybe you and Luca would like to come and visit sometime. Chance tells me it's beautiful country."

Pepper met her gaze again, and Cyn was shocked by how tired and forlorn her twin looked.

"I'll try, Cyn. But I just don't have it in me to hope for too much right now."

She nodded her head. There was really nothing more to say. Cyn turned and started toward the bedroom door.

"Cyn?" Her sister's voice was little more than a whisper.

She stopped, but found that she couldn't turn around and look back. If she did, she'd break down and cry.

"I am happy for you. I'm—sorry."

She nodded her head and walked out of the bedroom.

CHANCE LIKED LUCA just fine. Once you got to know him, he was really quite a guy.

He'd brought out some sort of Italian liqueur and had spiked their second cups of coffee. Chance had told him about seeing his video on television, and Luca had regaled him with a series of stories concerning the filming of those particular cooking classes. They'd laughed and drunk some more coffee.

They'd talked about the twins, and Chance had enjoyed hearing stories about their past.

Luca had even asked him several questions about the ranch, and expressed interest in coming out for a visit soon.

"That is," he said, taking another sip of his coffee, "if I can get that one upstairs out of the bedroom."

"You call us if you need anything. Anything at all." Chance's thoughts drifted back to his ranch and all the work he had waiting for him. Luca had seemed so interested in the daily operations of the ranch, he decided to continue the conversation.

"You know, sometimes you just have to approach things with a firm hand to make things go your way. You have to leave no room for chance."

"Tell me about it." Luca reached for another *biscotti* and settled back on the couch.

Chance could visualize the breeding center he and Mark had set up in the main barn. And he knew exactly the first of his prize cattle he wanted to place in the breeding stall, restrain, and impregnate with that championship bull sperm.

He took another sip of Luca's excellent coffee. It was probably Italian. "Luca, we wouldn't get half the results I expect for the future if we didn't have the means to simply strap that little gal in."

Luca's coffee cup stopped its ascent to his mouth.

Chance, so engrossed in thinking about how he was going to start his breeding program once he got back to the ranch, didn't notice his brother-in-law's change of expression.

"You—you strap her in?"

"Of course. How else do you think she'd remain still? She'd fight me all the way if I didn't restrain her. Sometimes it takes both me and my cousin using all our strength to get her into position."

Luca simply stared at him.

"I guess, to her, it's not that pleasant an experience, being impregnated."

"Hmm." Luca considered this. "You're sure there's no other alternative?"

"Positive. You know, we had one little gal that got so wild, she broke some of my equipment."

"Ohh." Luca set his coffee cup down and crossed his legs tightly. His face paled, and he set the half-eaten *biscotti* down in front of him.

"She . . . broke it?"

"Damaged the damn thing almost beyond repair. Boy, that was a painful moment. I was mad, let me tell you. Cost me a lot of money to get it fixed again and ready to do the job."

Luca swallowed, looking faintly nauseous. "I can understand."

"But, you know, it's all in a day's work. You have to take little accidents like that in stride."

"Why was she—so wild?"

"Hell, what I'm putting up her is so huge, it has to be pretty damn uncomfortable. The amount of noise she makes, I'm sure of it."

"I . . . see."

"Not that she has any choice in the matter. She's on my ranch, she gets impregnated."

"How lucky for her that she was so fertile before she got to the ranch."

"What?" Chance glanced at his brother-in-law and noticed the beads of sweat that had popped out on his forehead. "Luca, are you all right?"

"I have to say, Chance, that I admire you. You're quite a man."

"Luca, I think you might have—"

"Honey?" Cyn stood in the doorway, holding on to the doorframe as if she were going to fall. "Honey, I—"

Then she fainted.

SHE CAME TO and found herself lying on the living room couch, both Luca and Chance fussing over her.

"No wonder the poor little thing is so faint, what with you strapping her in and making her take that huge—"

"For God's sake, Luca, I was talking about my breeding program! I've never tied up a woman in my life!"

She had no idea what they were talking about and simply closed her eyes.

ON THE WAY HOME, Chance told her all about his and Luca's misunderstanding, and the two of them had a good laugh. She avoided talking about what happened with her twin, not sure if she could discuss it without bursting into tears.

Once back at her town house, she finished the last of her packing while Chance carried several filled boxes out to a storage space in the garage. They would come back for them later, he assured her. With a sister in Vegas, they would be visiting the city a few times a year.

If she'll even want to see me, Cyn thought.

They watched some television, then Cyn gave Chance a quick kiss on the cheek and headed for the stairs.

"Cyn?"

She was halfway up the flight of stairs and turned to look back down at him.

While she watched, he got up off the sofa. Something constricted in her chest as she watched him unfold his body from the couch, watched the way his muscles rippled. He was wearing well-worn jeans and his shirt was unbuttoned. She could see the clearly defined muscles in his abdomen.

"Yes?"

"I want to sleep with you."

She stood perfectly still. This part of their marriage still frightened her. Oh, she wasn't a virgin, that wasn't the point. What frightened her was the fact that she knew Chance would want more of her than any man ever had, before or since his explosion into her life.

She didn't know what to do.

"How do you feel about it?"

"Sleep . . . or sex?"

"We could start with sleeping and work our way up to sex."

She considered this.

"I thought that, well, when we got back to the ranch, we might have separate bedrooms for a while—"

"No."

He wasn't brutal about it, he simply made his decision very clear.

"Why not?"

"I don't want you growing away from me, Cyn. And I think that might happen if we had separate rooms."

"I see."

"Just sleep."

His negotiation for the night was quite clear. He wanted to sleep in the same bed with her. With any other man, she wouldn't have trusted him to keep his hands to himself. With Chance, she knew he would do the honorable thing.

"I'm not up to anything tonight, Chance."

"I know."

"I want to be very clear about that."

"I hear you."

Her heart was pounding so loudly she could barely hear her own voice.

"Come on up, then."

She turned and started up the stairs, supremely aware that he was right behind her.

She undressed for bed in the bathroom, donning a short nightgown and matching robe. After she slid between the sheets and turned off the lights, he went into the bathroom and took a shower. She kept her face averted into her pillow as she heard him walk back into the bedroom.

Then the mattress shifted as he sat down on it. She felt the covers move as he slipped beneath them. She lay perfectly still, not trusting herself and what she might want out of this man.

She waited. He was so still for so long she assumed he'd fallen asleep. When she shifted her weight to her elbows and started to turn around, she saw him. He was lying next to her on the bed. Her eyes had adjusted to the darkness of her bedroom, and she could see his eyes, see him looking at her. Studying her.

Before she had a chance to be nervous, he asked her a question. The deep, soft sound of his voice relaxed her.

"How did it go?"

She knew what he meant. Pepper.

"Badly."

He didn't say anything, waiting for her to go on.

"She's in so much pain, it was difficult to have a conversation with her."

He considered this, and while he did she adjusted her position in their bed so she was lying facing him.

"How did you feel?"

She sighed, and it felt like she was letting out a deep breath she'd kept inside her all night long.

"Horrible. I never meant to hurt her this way. But I also felt ... kind of angry."

"Yeah?"

He was so easy to talk to.

"Angry because ... I want to share this with her, my feelings, all the things I'm scared of. And I can't."

"Can you share them with me?"

"It's different."

He wasn't angry or upset, his ego didn't get in the way, and she was grateful for that.

"I feel like ... I've always been there for her, and now she isn't there for me. Like, when it comes to the things in my life, I'll always be alone."

The words were out of her mouth before she considered how they might sound. But Chance, so easygoing, so solid and secure, didn't take offense.

"You aren't alone anymore," he whispered against her hair.

She put her arms around him, then kissed him goodnight.

"No. I'm not."

Chapter Eight

The C & M Ranch exceeded her wildest expectations.

When Chance had said ranch, she had expected a ranch-style house out on a couple of acres, maybe a few horses like Mr. Ed in the barn, some cattle and a few fields of hay. Chickens by the corral, a couple of cats. Maybe even a goat.

The C & M was a world unto itself.

Chance and his cousin hadn't been fooling around. The C & M Ranch encompassed seven thousand acres. And on those acres were *hundreds* of cattle.

Chance lived and worked on the ranch, and spent a great deal of his time on a horse, a huge pinto named Pancho. Pancho liked her instantly, which Chance said was a good sign.

The C & M was located just outside of Sheridan, on the eastern slopes of the Bighorn Mountains in northern Wyoming. They arrived at the ranch late that first night, and Cyn had seen little of the place. Chance had hustled her inside. She'd barely been able to take a look at the large ranch house before being rushed off to bed.

She'd been touched at Chance's thoughtfulness. Apparently he'd called Eunice, because there was an obviously new quilt on the bed, along with a vase full of wildflowers on the nightstand. The master bedroom was a large room, but still gave the impression of being cozy.

But the bed was smaller than the other one they'd shared. That first night, she didn't have time for any fears, as she was exhausted. Her head hit the pillow, and when she woke up the next morning, she was alone.

The quality of the light told her it was just after sunrise. Chance, her new husband, had already started his day.

She wasn't exactly sure what she was supposed to do with herself. Getting out of bed, she'd headed toward the window and then stopped. The sheer, majestic beauty of the land hit her, and she walked slowly toward the window and looked outside.

Mountains, craggy and high, could be seen in the distance. Trees, green and lush, were everywhere. She wasn't sure what kind they were, but the landscape was totally different from the desert that had been her home.

The colors were more vivid, it felt wilder. It even *smelled* wilder.

She found a note on the bedside table.

Honey,
Sleep in, then take your time getting to know the house. Eunice will be there if you need anything. I'll be back late tonight, around seven, for dinner. See you then.

C

There was nothing he expected her to do. She didn't know what she was supposed to do. For someone who had been supremely responsible all of her adult life, it was a totally foreign experience.

And rather liberating.

As she showered, she thought about her new life. And especially about the baby. So far, she hadn't experienced any of the normal morning sickness. In fact, her doctor had pronounced her disgustingly healthy. Her breasts were fuller, and she was more easily tired, but except for the bottle of prenatal vitamins she now carried in her purse, no one would have suspected she would be a mother by Christmas.

Once her shower was complete, Cyn found her suitcase and pulled out clean clothing. She'd done a little shopping before coming to the ranch, picking up the sorts of clothes she assumed people wore out West. Today, she dressed in jeans and a pale mint, short-sleeved shirt. After lacing up her sneakers, she started down the stairs.

A black Labrador looked up from his spot on a hooked rug in the hallway and gave her a halfhearted woof.

"That's just Bruce's way of saying hello," said a voice.

She stopped on the stairs, unsure.

"Hello?"

"Come on into the kitchen and I'll fix you some breakfast."

That voice had to belong to Eunice. It was scratchy and sharp, and the woman matched her vocal tones.

Cyn was reminded of Rosalind Russell, for this woman was a no-nonsense, take-no-prisoners type of gal.

"Pancakes, waffles or eggs?"

Cyn was astounded at the variety offered. It was like having your own Denny's at your disposal.

"Waffles."

"Bacon or sausage?"

"Bacon."

"Toast?"

"No, thank you."

"Orange juice?"

"I'd love some."

She'd brought her purse down with her, and Cyn saw Eunice catch her eye as she shook out a prenatal vitamin and took it with a healthy swallow of juice.

"My, my," the older woman said softly. "Well, congratulations. It's about time that big guy got himself a wife and started working on filling this old ranch house with a few kids."

"Thank you." To her complete and utter embarrassment, Cyn's eyes filled with tears. These were the words she'd been longing to hear from her sister, from her mother, from another woman. That they should have to be delivered by an almost total stranger saddened her.

"Here now, we can't have you crying on a beautiful day like this." Eunice wiped her hands on her apron, then pulled up a chair alongside her. "Don't worry, honey, every woman gets a little emotional when she's about to bring life into the world."

This only made Cyn cry harder.

"Oh, you poor little thing." Eunice enfolded her in her strong, wiry arms, and Cyn simply leaned into the embrace, too overwhelmed with feeling to fight it.

When she'd finished sobbing, Eunice handed her a handful of tissues, then slapped down a plate with one perfect, golden waffle on it and four slices of bacon.

"You eat all that, you hear?"

Cyn smiled, then picked up her fork. In her most private fantasies as a little girl, she'd longed for a mother to look after her. Now it seemed she might get her wish, for Eunice was surely a tough old mother hen.

Once breakfast was finished, she let the housekeeper outline their day.

"Chance asked me to show you around the house. He told me to tell you that you can change whatever you want, even knock out the walls if it'll make you happy."

She laughed at that and patted the top of Bruce's head. He was now her new best friend after she'd snuck him two slices of bacon. He gave her a doggy grin and wagged his tail.

The ranch house was large, solid and well built. But to Cyn, it felt neglected. In her days as a Realtor, she'd secretly imagined that each house she showed had a personality. And they did. You could feel it if you simply stood silently and listened.

This ranch house might be the strong, silent type, but it felt neglected nonetheless.

Downstairs housed the kitchen, Chance's office, a bathroom, a large living room, a dining room, and in the far back what she supposed was a family room.

Cyn took in the space with her Realtor's eye, already thinking of ways to brighten up the rooms and bring more of a family feel to them.

A large porch dominated the front of the house, and she was pleased with the porch swing and several chairs that had been set out on the weathered planks.

"It's beautiful," she told Eunice.

"Huh!" the woman said, almost with a snort. Then she smiled. "You'll do."

Cyn thought that was a strange thing to say, but kept her silence.

Upstairs there were four bedrooms including the master bedroom, and two other bathrooms, as well. Cyn grew quiet as they entered one of the smaller bedrooms.

"Perfect for a nursery, wouldn't you say?" said Eunice, almost reading her thoughts.

"It would be." Cyn wondered how forthcoming the housekeeper might be, and decided to jump right in.

"Why did Chance say I could change anything I wanted?"

Eunice gave her a long look, as if assessing her character. Finally, she spoke up.

"That first gal he married, Annie, wasn't worth much. She bitched and moaned about how bored she was. How isolated ranch life was. I guess she thought she could've done better, but I didn't think so. In my opinion, she wasn't good enough for him.

"That boy did everything he could do to please her, but in the end they got a divorce and she ruined Chance financially."

Cyn took all this in, considering.

"So they never lived here. I mean, she never did."

"No, ma'am."

"This is his second ranch."

"His third. The first belonged to his Daddy, but he liked his liquor too well and lost all his land. I think Chance was just a little boy when that happened."

They had more in common than Cyn had thought, she and her husband.

Eunice cleared her throat and Cyn glanced at the woman. "Well, to answer your original question? My guess would be that he wants you to be happy here."

"I am happy." Cyn, at that moment, decided to trust Eunice. "I'm happy with him."

"It can get lonely here for a woman."

"I'm not easily bored."

"You're a smart one, I can see that."

"Eunice," Cyn said, thinking through her choice of words carefully, "what do you think I could choose to do that would make Chance happiest?"

Eunice finally smiled, and the expression crinkled the corners of her eyes and lit them from within.

"Oh, little girl, I've been waiting for you for a long time. I couldn't be fonder of that boy if he was my own. He deserves some happiness after what he's been through.

"You want to know what would make him happy? Make him a home. Make this place over and fill it with children. Give Chance a taste of the family he's waited his entire life for."

At that moment, Cyn knew she had a good chance of making her marriage succeed. For she and Chance wanted exactly the same thing.

"Would you help me? With the planning and everything?"

Eunice wiggled her eyebrows and actually laughed. "I wouldn't have it any other way."

THEY SPENT THE MORNING in the kitchen, plotting and planning.

"I want to do the family room first. It's one of the most neglected, and it's out of the way so we can work on it without disrupting the rest of the house."

Eunice nodded her head as she studied her sketches. "We can hire Andy's boys to come help with the heavy work. We'll have to move a lot of that old furniture out, do some scrubbing and painting—"

"New carpet—"

"Curtains—"

The day flew by, and dinner was on the table before Cyn knew what had happened.

"Cookie and Chance will be here in about half an hour. You just run on up and make yourself pretty for him."

Cyn was surprised at how much she had come to like this old woman in a single afternoon. "I think I'll do that."

She hurried up the stairs, and as she approached the bedroom, Cyn decided on a shower. She'd spent most of the afternoon taking measurements of the family room, moving the smaller articles of furniture, and now her muscles were slightly sore. A hot shower would fix that.

Inside the bathroom, she slipped off her clothing and was about to step inside the shower stall when she caught sight of herself in the mirror.

The pregnancy was going to transform her body. As she studied her reflection, a thought crept into her mind. She wondered if Chance would find her body attractive.

She knew the answer to that. He was definitely attracted to her, and had told her he had been from the start. She was the one who was putting their sexual life on hold. Tonight, when they went to bed, would he expect her to want to make love? How long could they go on sleeping in the same bed and not having a sex life?

With a man like Chance? Not for long. Cyn stared at herself in the mirror and decided that tonight was going to be the night. It wasn't fair to Chance, to make him wait for what any other husband would enjoy on a regular basis. Part of making their house a home included both emotional and sexual bonding. If she wasn't the most talented woman he'd ever been to bed with, well, she'd make sure he taught her exactly what it was he wanted.

How strange, to feel she was in competition with herself. With the woman who had been hypnotized to be insatiable.

She wasn't sure how long she stood there before scooping her clothing up off the floor and tossing it into the hamper. Then she pulled her hair up on top of her head with a rubber band and stepped into the shower stall, closing the frosted glass door behind her.

Cyn was about to turn on the water when she heard a noise in the bedroom. Thinking it might be Eunice, coming to tell her dinner was ready and the men were already at the table, Cyn curled her fingers around the shower stall's doorknob.

She was about to open the stall door and grab a bath towel when the bathroom door swung open and Chance stepped inside.

She froze.

He'd kicked off his boots and didn't have his hat on, but now she watched as he swiftly unbuttoned his shirt and pulled it off his chest. Cyn knew she should say something, make some sort of noise, alert him to her presence in the bathroom. But she couldn't seem to make her body respond.

She simply watched. Watched as her husband tossed his sweaty shirt into the hamper, then unfastened his jeans and pushed them down over his hips, along with his briefs.

She'd never seen him naked. Well, she had. Brief moments. But only when she'd been so nervous she hadn't had a chance to really look at him.

He was beautiful.

The glass door to the shower stall had a floral design made up of both etched and clear glass, and now Cyn peeked through a patch of clear glass and spied on her naked husband.

Chance turned on the tap, then splashed water over his face. He looked tired. Exhausted. Dirty and sweaty and overworked. Cyn felt a rush of compassion for him. It had to be tough, coming back to a ranch that needed so much work, a ranch he'd neglected while helping her straighten out her life. Now he was trying to catch up, and he was obviously a hard worker.

The C & M meant so much to him.

She studied his body. Tough and hard and roped with muscles. Scars. She counted three or four, the ridged puckering lines contrasting sharply against his deep, sun-darkened skin. His hands were callused. Weathered from years and years in the saddle and in the sun. Holding reins and fixing fence lines. She'd felt those hands on her before, and she wanted to feel them against her skin now.

She knew he would head for the shower shortly, would find her there. Would know what she'd been doing.

The thought of being discovered was highly arousing. She knew that this time, no matter what she said or how she might protest, he wouldn't stop. She didn't want him to. On a certain, primitive, feminine level, she wanted this particular decision taken out of her hands.

She also knew there was only so far you could push a man. It was one thing to say you weren't going to have sex when you were both dressed and headed up to bed, or when you were beneath the covers in pajamas. But to tell your own husband you refused to have sex with him when you were both naked and highly aroused—

He turned off the tap, then reached for one of the towels and dried his face. She watched as he took a deep breath and knew she had to tell him now, let him know she was in the bathroom with him, if she had any hope of escaping without a sexual encounter.

She didn't want to tell him anything. She wanted him to discover her. She watched, her heart in her throat, as he turned from the sink and headed toward the shower.

He was outside the shower stall now, she'd backed up and could see the outline of his big body against the frosted glass. Then she heard the door start to click open, then he stepped inside, and then—

Then he saw her.

His hand froze on its way to turning on the shower. He simply looked down at her. She couldn't read the expression on his face. Then she noticed the infinitesimal hardening of his facial muscles, the narrowing of his dark blue eyes.

"Cyn?" he said, and her stomach muscles quivered at the sound of his voice.

She wet her lips with the tip of her tongue and tried to find her breath. He watched her, and stole it right back.

"Cyn?" Now he was reaching for her, and she knew all was lost. She wanted all to be lost. She wanted to make love to this man, her husband, while she was fully conscious, and she wanted to give him everything she was capable of giving to a man.

His hand stopped before he reached her, as if for just an instant he was unsure. But his body wasn't. What his mind might have wanted to forestall, his body was incapable of stopping. She was aware of his body, of the rapid lengthening and thickening of his sex, of the desperate control he was attempting to exert.

She made the decision for both of them, stepping into his arms, putting one hand on the back of his neck and bringing his lips down over hers, putting her other hand around his rigid arousal.

He kissed her like a starving man seated at a banquet—without restraint, with heat and passion and force. His grip on her almost hurt. Then, as if he realized she was the smaller and softer of the two of them, the pressure of his fingers softened. He pulled her hard against him, pressing their bodies together as he continued to kiss her.

Any fears she had were wiped away in that instant. Hypnosis or not, they were meant for each other. Whether you wanted to attribute attraction like this to pheromones or hormones, or claim it was fated by the stars, heat like this between a man and a woman was nothing short of a miracle.

She touched him with a surer hand and he moaned against her mouth. His hands moved over her breasts, her waist, her hips, her buttocks, touching, pleasing, caressing. She thought he might turn on the shower, but he surprised her by stepping out of the stall and taking her with him.

She watched, in a sensual daze, as he approached the bathroom door and locked it. Then he reached inside the shower stall and turned on the water, then shut the door. They stood just outside the shower, on a plush area rug, as hot water beat down and began to fill the bathroom with steam.

"They'll think we're taking a shower together," he whispered.

"Aren't we going to?"

"No. What I want to do to you can't be done as well inside a shower stall."

She understood his intent when he lowered her down onto the rug. He didn't waste time with a lot of preliminaries, and she didn't need them. He simply positioned her on the rug, pushed her thighs apart and slid between them. She put her arms around his neck and closed her eyes.

She'd seen his sex, and been intimidated by its size, but nothing prepared her for the feeling of exquisite pleasure that shook her body when he entered her. Cyn's eyes flew open and she cried out.

"Easy," he whispered, then set a steady, slow rhythm.

She twisted her head from side to side on the thick rug. "No," she whispered against his ear.

"What do you want?"

"Do it the way you want to." When he hesitated, she said, "You won't hurt me."

His thrusts became stronger, and she raised her hips to meet his downward strokes. He continued kissing and caressing her as he filled her, and she was so full of a trembling kind of emotion that she felt tears sliding out of her eyes and down the sides of her face.

She couldn't concentrate on him or what he was doing anymore. Cyn fell back against the rug, her arms going slack, not holding him against her naked, sweat-slicked body. He was relentless as he moved above her, his hips pumping strongly, his powerful erection sliding in and out of her.

She'd never felt this way before, as if she were reaching for something in the midst of a burning, white-hot heat. Her skin felt too sensitized, her breasts too full, then he reached beneath her and cupped her buttocks, pulling her more sharply against his rigid length—

She shattered, into countless, pulsing pieces. She cried out at that moment, and he followed her into her sensual descent. She barely felt his climax, she was too wrapped up in her own.

When he finally slid off her, when she finally let him go, he sat up and pulled her into his lap, facing him, her legs spread over his thighs.

He kissed her, again and again, and she felt desire pulse swiftly between her legs even though she was so very sore.

"Did I hurt you?" he whispered.

"No." She kissed his cheek, then his chin, then his lips. "No, you were wonderful."

"And you . . . did you?"

She knew he only asked her because she'd been so afraid that nothing would happen. This had nothing to do with his masculine ego, and everything to do with his wanting to make her happy. She couldn't stop smiling.

"Ba-boom. Every time."

He lowered her down onto the rug and they simply lay there for a while, side by side, the water running in the shower, the mirror all steamed up. She snuggled against him, enjoyed the feel of his large hands running up and down her spine, over her hips, her breasts, her thighs.

He eased her over onto her back, cupped one of her breasts with his hand, and lowered his mouth to the hard nipple.

"Oh!" She almost came up off the rug when he pulled the tip of her breast into his mouth. She moved beneath him, restless again, restless and wanting.

He pleasured her while taking pleasure in her body, lavishing time and care on both her breasts, her belly, her inner thighs, and finally to that sweetness that was the center of her sexuality. He made her respond that way, shatter again before he slid back up her body and sheathed himself deeply inside her sensitized flesh once again.

And this time it was slow, so slow, and so very sexual. He moved inside her until she was frantic with need, and watched as she tumbled over into that total feminine release.

She had to rest for a moment after that, and she couldn't think of a better way of resting, with Chance's big body pinning her to the bathroom floor. He felt so good against her, inside her, with her. She looked up into his blue eyes and knew she'd finally come home.

Cyn raised her head so her lips were close to his ear.

"Did you come?"

He shook his head.

"Well that's no fun."

"It's a lot of fun watching you. Honey, where did you get the idea you were cold in bed?"

She smiled and stretched beneath him, then closed her eyes against his intense scrutiny. "Maybe I never met the right man." She kissed his ear, then whispered, "Maybe I ought to send Madame Babala a thank-you note."

He laughed.

She lay back against the rug and this time she looked right up at him, wanting to gauge his reaction.

"I've never responded like that, not even hypnotically."

He nodded his head. "This is a lot better."

"For me, too."

He kissed her forehead. "I'm glad."

She shifted beneath him. "We'll run out of hot water."

He smiled. "Did you plan on taking a shower?"

"Won't it be kind of rude not to show up for dinner?"

"I told Eunice if we weren't down in around fifteen minutes to put our dinners in the fridge. We'll heat them up later."

"So they know what we're up to."

"Does that embarrass you?"

She shrugged. "Nah. It's what newlyweds are supposed to do, isn't it?"

He moved against her, starting that familiar, tantalizing stroking all over again. Then he lowered his face until his lips were barely brushing hers before he whispered, "My thoughts exactly."

Chapter Nine

If someone had told Chance before his trip how his life was going to change in a matter of weeks, he wouldn't have believed it. From a man who had gone to Las Vegas with a mission in mind, who had also hit the bars with the express purpose of having a bit of uncomplicated sexual fun, he'd become a married man who couldn't wait to get home every night.

It wasn't that he loved his ranch less. The work still consumed him. There was always something that had to be done. Working cattle, fixing fences, baling hay or just troubleshooting. A rancher simply did what had to be done. There was no such thing as a set routine at the C & M, every day was different. Though it was a sunup to sundown kind of job, seven days a week, Chance had realized a long time ago that the independent, unpredictable qualities of his workday made up a large part of what he loved about being a rancher.

And it was quite similar to the myriad feelings he had for his new bride, as well.

Cyn was completely unpredictable. He never knew exactly what to expect when he arrived home, and that was a large part of what intrigued him. She wasn't the typical rancher's wife, that was clear. Eunice had already told him she was something of a disaster in the kitchen. Her biscuits, though well intentioned, could've been used as hockey pucks, but everyone was far too kind to tell her so. Cyn had figured it out when even the pigs had turned them down, and she'd left the kitchen in Eunice's capable hands.

Now each time he thought of her—and he thought of her often as he sat astride Pancho's back, riding the fence line or working with the cattle—she brought a smile to his lips. She was always up to something, and had recently told him she was in the process of renovating the family room at the back of the ranch house. He'd told her not to exhaust herself, that her main job was to simply settle in and get used to ranch life, take care of herself and her pregnancy. Their pregnancy. Their baby.

But she was a whirlwind, and Chance was glad she'd thrown herself into this marriage with such enthusiasm.

It wasn't just their physical relationship that lured him home, though that was spectacular enough that it would have cut short his days in itself. It was Cyn. He liked seeing her smile, making her laugh, hearing about her day and sharing his with her. He just liked her. And that, after his unfortunate marriage to Annie, was a great comfort to him.

He loved her, he knew that now. He loved her in a way he'd never approached loving his first wife, and he did everything in his power to let her know this, trying to think of different ways he could pleasure her, make her happy. Chance lived in silent fear that the novelty of the ranch would wear off and Cyn would become bored, but at the same time he wasn't really worried. She wouldn't be able to redecorate the entire ranch before their baby arrived, and motherhood would keep her busy.

Yet he thought she might be the sort of woman who would need something of her own besides home and hearth. She'd been a Realtor in Las Vegas, but she'd confided in him that she'd grown bored with that job long before she'd left it. He had no idea if she'd ever had any dreams or aspirations beyond selling properties. He knew she'd given up any sort of dream to take care of herself and her twin. To survive.

Well, she didn't have to merely survive anymore. She had him, and he would make sure her life was as happy as he could possibly make it. It would be his secret mission, to keep his wife so happy she'd never want to leave.

HE LEFT THE BARN that evening at sunset, stopping for a moment to admire the colors in the sky. Chance loved working outside, feeling that he was part of the land, part of a great process. Looking at the sunset reinforced that feeling for him in an almost spiritual manner.

A particular kind of calm had settled over him when he resumed his walk to the ranch house—until he saw his wife's silhouette up on the roof.

"Cyn?" he shouted, concern etching his voice. "Cyn? What are you doing up there?"

He heard her muffled curse, then the slight hesitation before she called down to him, "You weren't supposed to be home this early."

"Damn straight," he muttered as he ran to the side of the house and started to climb the sturdy trellis to the roof. "What the hell are you doing up there?"

"It was supposed to be a surprise!" she wailed.

"It's a surprise. You surprised me right out of my socks. Does Eunice know you're up here?" He was on the roof and walking to her side when he stopped in his tracks.

Cyn, dressed in jeans and a striped T-shirt, had been in the middle of adjusting a satellite dish. It was one of the newer models, small and compact, not unwieldy at all.

She dusted her hands off on her jeans. "I meant to have it all up and ready by the time you got home. I thought you might like to see something on television besides the farm report."

He had to smile in spite of the concern he'd had for her. The roof of the farmhouse was actually quite manageable once you got up on top of it. He could see which bedroom window she'd climbed out of in order to position the dish.

"Does Eunice know about this?"

"She drove into town with me to pick it up."

He nodded his head. "What are you doing now?"

"Well, I just finished drilling a few holes in the roof and fastening it into place, and I just have to adjust the dish and pick up the signal."

His wife. He couldn't get over her.

"Want some help?"

She wrinkled her nose as she looked up at him. "I would think you'd want a hot shower and a good meal before getting involved with something like this."

"What's for dinner?"

"Eunice's beef stew."

"Did you help?"

She punched his arm. "Yeah, I asked her if I could make you a few biscuits."

He pulled her into his arms and kissed the top of her head. "They weren't that bad."

"Don't lie to me." Her voice was muffled against his chest, but he could hear the laughter in it.

"Okay, they were that bad. How's about if I help you with the dish, then we can both take a shower—"

"And miss dinner again—"

"No, no, hear me out. I'll make it a point of honor to keep my hands off you. I'll simply admire you—"

"I'm getting fat, Chance."

"You are not."

"My stomach is starting to pooch out."

"Really?" Everything about her fascinated him, and now his hands found their way beneath her T-shirt.

"Okay, maybe just a little." The fact that she carried his child fascinated him.

"I can't fit into any of my old clothes."

"Buy new ones."

"I don't want to run up all these bills."

"I want you to be comforta—"

"Are you two going to get that damn dish adjusted, or am I supposed to sit in the family room all day and just hope a clear signal will eventually come through?"

They both jumped as Eunice appeared at the window.

"Eunice! Oh, no, I'm sorry, I wasn't thinking—"

"I've noticed you don't do a lot of thinking when that cowboy's around. Chance, what are you doing up on the roof?"

"I saw her up here and came to investigate."

"Huh." Eunice snorted in a most inelegant manner, her gaze taking in his hands beneath Cyn's T-shirt. "Uh-huh. Well, let's get this baby in place, I've got a stew to attend to." Despite the gruffness of her voice, Chance could make out the amused twinkle in her hazel eyes. "I suppose the two of you won't be down for dinner." She held up her hands before he could reply.

"Never mind. I'll leave two plates warming in the oven."

THE SATELLITE DISH was a great success, as was the family room. Once they had the dish locked on to the signal, Cyn let Chance come in and investigate what she'd been up to for the past several weeks.

He couldn't believe it was the same room. Rag rugs had been taken up and cleaned, the wooden floor polished to a high gloss. The walls had been painted a pale yellow, and the warm color was exactly right for a room that would have to withstand cold winters.

She and Eunice had spent a lot of time arguing over window treatments, but as far as Chance could see, the curtains worked just fine. Several pieces of new furniture had been added, and as their bank balance hadn't dipped drastically, he knew she'd purchased them out of her own savings account.

A huge couch dominated the center of the room, along with several comfortable chairs. He recognized Eunice's handiwork in the two crocheted afghans draped over the couch. The colors were all golds and rusts and browns, earthy colors, nature colors.

He was speechless.

There had been a box of pictures in his office, various cattle and horses that had graced the C & M over the first few years of its operation. She'd had them matted and framed, and now instead of languishing, hidden, in the closet in his office, they graced the walls. There was a dried flower arrangement in a brass teapot by the stone fireplace, and several framed photos on the mantel.

He walked slowly through the room, aware that she was watching his every move. His throat closed with emotion as Chance realized that his dream of having a real home wasn't that far from his grasp.

He turned to face her. "You did a great job." The minute the words were out of his mouth, he felt they were inadequate. He wasn't good with words, or talking. Communication, Cookie said. He taped "Oprah" every day because he liked watching folks settle their problems. In the morning, over coffee, he'd regale them with what he'd seen the night before.

According to Cookie, what women wanted were the words. Those fancy words he didn't seem capable of coming up with. But he had to try, because Cyn had put so much of herself into this room, and had done it for him.

He cleared his throat. "Cyn."

She was watching him. Smiling.

He thought of the best way to communicate what he was feeling. "I'm...overwhelmed."

The smile grew bigger. She came to his side, took his hand, led him over to the largest chair.

"This one's yours."

He sat down in it, and she showed him how it could be maneuvered, how he could lean back and the footrest would shoot out. How he could put his feet up after a hard day's work.

"And," she said, still glowing with pride and clearly happy with her work, "with the curtains back, there's quite a view."

There was, indeed. The windows, formerly dusty with neglect, now sparkled. Outside, you could see mountains in the distance, and trees so green they appeared almost to have a bluish haze.

Words weren't enough. He pulled her into his lap and heard her laugh as she came down on top of him. Her cheek felt exactly right against his chest, and Chance felt a great wave of contentment wash over him.

Maybe, right at this particular moment, words weren't necessary after all.

THE BELL RANG sharply in the kitchen, and the two women jumped.

"That man," said Eunice with a smile, "never used to come by the house several times a day."

"Hmm," was all Cyn said in reply, but she couldn't stop the smile forming on her face as she walked to the back door. Chance was standing there, three large cardboard boxes by his feet.

"These were at the post office for you," he said as he walked into the kitchen carrying the largest one.

"You don't have mud on those boots, do you?" Eunice yelped.

Cyn almost laughed out loud. The bell that rang in the kitchen served as a warning to both Eunice and herself that there was a cowboy outside who needed something. In rainy or muddy weather, or simply while working with the animals, a cowboy's boots could get quite dirty. Eunice had thought of having the bell installed years ago, claiming that it took years off her workload not to have to scrub the kitchen floor almost every day.

"No, ma'am, they're clean. I just came back from town."

"Did you find the part for the truck?"

"Yes, ma'am." Chance set the large box down by the back door.

Eunice gave him a good long stare. "And the fact that I'm making my apple pie had nothing to do with you hanging around my kitchen?"

"Not at all. Though Cookie did say he'd be much obliged if you'd save an extra big piece for his dinner."

She snorted, then went back to peeling apples.

Cyn followed her husband outside, where the other two boxes still sat. She reached for one, but Chance forestalled her.

"Don't pick that up!"

"Chance," she said, working her way into the phrases she said several times a day. "Pregnancy is not a disease and I'm not an invalid—"

Her sentence was cut off as he covered her mouth with his, kissing her in a way that made her forget her own name.

She'd decided several weeks ago that their marriage had a damn good chance of working. Their physical compatibility was extraordinary, and she figured that by the time that wore off, they might possibly have learned to appreciate other things about each other, or at least be able to talk to each other.

But for now, this was just fine.

She moved closer against him, then gave up all pretense of impartiality and jumped up, twining her long, jeans-clad legs around his waist.

He groaned, deep in his throat, and continued kissing her.

When he finally stopped, she rested her forehead against his. She was still in his arms, and had absolutely no fear that he would drop her.

"What are your plans for today?" he whispered.

"I thought I might see what was in these boxes, then do a little work in the nursery."

He nodded his head. "I'll help."

"Chance, you have to fix the truck—"

"Cookie will give me half an hour."

She narrowed her eyes to mere slits and gave him a look. "It never takes you less than half an hour."

"I'll time myself. You can time me—"

"A quickie, huh?"

"I'm a desperate man."

"That's the truth." She wriggled out of his arms and set her feet on the ground. "I'm taking that smaller box and carrying it up to the bedroom."

"I'll be right behind you."

He followed her into the kitchen, and as they passed through, Cyn called out to Eunice, "We'll just take these upstairs and get them out of your way—"

Eunice gave them both a look out of her shrewd hazel eyes that said she knew exactly what was going on, then resumed peeling her apples.

"SHE DOESN'T TRUST me, Pancho."

Chance was checking out one of the C & M's irrigation systems as he talked with his pinto gelding. Pancho was one of the ranch's finest horses. He had a superb temperament, gentle and steady, but responsive and sensitive. Chance would've bet money on the fact that this animal understood every word he said. The gentle brown eyes were compassionate as they stared at him, and Chance continued talking as he worked.

"She does on a certain level. She knows I'm going to be good to her. And it's not about her having her own money, her own account. That's not it. It's just that— she keeps a part of herself separate, and I'm not even sure if it has anything to do with me."

Pancho stared at Chance steadily, and, encouraged by his mount's attentiveness, Chance continued.

"She's been on her own for so long, depended on herself for so long, it's as if—she doesn't know how to give it over to another person." He swallowed against the tightness in his throat. "Perhaps she never will, Pancho. But you know what? It doesn't matter. I think what I have to do is simply remember my wedding vows. I made a promise to love her, and that's just what I'll have to do. Not like that's any kind of real effort for me," he added hastily. "It's not like I have to force myself to do it, or anything."

Pancho snorted gently in response.

"You're the only person I can talk to about this. Eunice might understand, but I couldn't see dragging her into something so private. Cookie would have a lot of advice for me. Hell, he'd probably write Oprah a letter with an idea for another show. 'Ranchers who can't talk to their wives.'"

Chance laughed, then reached out and patted Pancho's long, smooth neck. The gelding leaned into the caress, as both man and horse were totally comfortable with each other after years of a working relationship.

"I have to admire you, Pancho. You have whole herds of females—well, not anymore, but I mean you would if you'd grown up in the wild."

Pancho snorted companionably, not at all put out by Chance's mistake.

"You handle whole herds, and I can't even get a handle on one female."

Pancho snorted again.

"You're right. I'll just have to give it time, see what happens. Maybe—maybe once the baby comes, she'll learn that she doesn't have to stand all alone, that she can depend on me."

He thought of the beautiful family room, and of the nursery Cyn was now concentrating on decorating. And Chance knew, in his heart, that it took a lot more than redecorating a ranch house to make it into a home.

He hadn't even realized how much he wanted it all until Cyn had burst into his life. He did want it all—he wanted all of her. He wanted her to be able to trust him completely, to love him absolutely. He wanted her trust, he wanted her to know, on a soul-deep level, that he would always be there for her.

And he wondered, at various moments during his workday, if that would ever happen. If she would ever let it happen.

Finished with his check, Chance got back up in the saddle and headed toward the south pasture.

SHE SAT IN THE FAMILY room and concentrated on the baby afghan that was slowly taking shape in her hands.

Eunice had taken the time to teach her the basics, and had even loaned her a booklet with all the techniques illustrated, including this particular pattern for a baby afghan. Now, looking at the tangle of pastel yarn in front of her, Cyn wondered if she'd be able to accomplish this latest task she'd set for herself.

She set the yarn and the crochet hook down and glanced around the familiar room. She'd done a good job, and she knew Chance had been pleased. Now, in the evenings, they spent time down here, watching television, reading, playing cards. Laughing. He never bored her. She loved to ask about his day, and he always obliged. She found that she was proud of her husband, of the work he did, of the things he accomplished. She liked the man he was.

Chance had shown her, in so many ways, that he was a man who could be trusted. Yet she knew there was a part of her heart that might never be his, and she hated herself for it. Cyn had never found it easy to trust in people, to trust that they would be there for her if she needed them.

Much of the time, they hadn't been. She'd grown up depending on herself, and that was what she was comfortable with. Now, having Chance to lean on, she found the whole experience disconcerting. Disquieting. It made her uneasy.

He wasn't a stupid man. He knew. She'd realized it within the first month she'd come to live in his house. Chance was a man who was attuned to a deeper rhythm in life. He was surrounded by nature all the time, and noticed nature's subtleties. When he was home, he noticed things about her that an ordinary man might not pay any attention to.

Chance was far from an ordinary man.

He knew she held back, and as he gave her so much, she felt doubly guilty. But she didn't know what else to do, because she certainly didn't want to pretend to have feelings that weren't there.

Stop being so hard on yourself.

She picked up the hook again, then set it down. Restless, she wandered up to the master bedroom and began rummaging through the three boxes she'd received in the mail a few days ago.

They had all been from Deva, a kind of belated wedding gift and a thank you for subletting her the town house in Las Vegas. Two of the boxes had been filled with books. New Age subjects, of course. Everything from aromatherapy to reflexology, from meditation to homeopathic medicine. There had even been several health food cookbooks.

Cyn had shelved them all on the bookshelves in her bedroom. She'd been touched by Deva's generosity, and even laughed when she'd discovered that one of the books had been a discussion of the uses of hypnosis. Several had covered healthy pregnancy and childbirth, and she knew she'd have a lot of reading material once the weather turned cooler.

She'd opened the third box, but hadn't managed to find a place for its various contents. Essential oils and teas, massage lotions and soaps, even a few crystals. Deva had gone over the top, and Cyn had a sinking feeling that the sensitive woman had thought to compensate for Pepper's absence in her life.

Cyn missed her twin terribly, but there was nothing she could do. She'd left a few messages on Pepper's machine, and now it was up to her sister to make some sort of contact. She couldn't force the issue.

Wanting to take her mind off the subject, Cyn turned her attention to unpacking the third box. The oils caught her interest, and she uncapped several of them and sniffed them. Such wonderful smells—rose, lavender, geranium, cinnamon and nutmeg. A few she wasn't familiar with, like tea tree and chamomile. But they caught her interest, as did the paperback book on the various uses of the oils.

Her interest piqued, she carried the oils and the book down to the kitchen and set them on the table. Eunice was making lemonade, but she stopped what she was doing and came over and sat down.

"What are you up to?"

"Smell some of these, they're wonderful! There's a chapter in this book on using oils to make a house more fragrant."

"Couldn't hurt. Especially in the winter."

Something in the table of contents caught Cyn's eye, and she whispered, "Eunice, look at this! Natural Health for Domestic Animals. I wonder if that includes cattle and horses...."

"Uh-oh—"

"Arthritic dog treatment," Cyn said, reading from the book. "Listen to this! There's a recipe for a dog toothpaste and breath deodorizer."

"You are something," Eunice replied. "I've never heard of half the things you talk about."

"Organic flea collars—"

"That would come in handy for poor Bruce—"

"I never liked those chemical things, the way they smell—oh, there's a whole section on cows, bulls and calves—"

"Now, honey, maybe I'd ask Chance before I'd go experimenting—"

"None of this hurts them, it just seems to—" Cyn paused as she read. "It's like a tonic."

Eunice couldn't repress her smile. "Then you go right ahead, honey. Those cattle won't know what hit them."

"WHAT'S THAT SMELL?" Cookie demanded.

"What smell?" Chance replied.

"Can't you smell it? Not that I'm complaining, it's a helluva lot better than what this barn usually smells like."

"It *is* different. Damn. Strange, but not unpleasant."

They looked at each other as the thought came to each man at the same time.

"Cyn."

"FENNEL AND CHAMOMILE?"

"It's a tonic, Chance. I didn't put it in their feed, I would never do anything like that without your express permission. But I thought the cows might feel better if their barn smelled a little more pleasant."

"Cattle don't care how they smell."

"How do you know? Maybe they do! And did you know that adding one drop of chamomile to a calves' feed can help if they have diarrhea—"

"Cyn. I really appreciate your concern with the well-being of our cattle. But it's just that I'd appreciate it a lot more if you'd tell me what you're up to before you do it. It just—caught me by surprise, that's all." He didn't dare tell her that the men were hooting and hollering out in the bunkhouse. His wife would be crushed to know that several of the cowboys who worked the C & M thought she was just plain nuts.

"Okay. But before you think this is all just a bunch of bunk, can I try an experiment with Pancho?"

He thought for a moment, then nodded his head. "What?"

"I know you really love that horse. I know you talk to him—"

"What?"

"I came looking for you in the stable, but the two of you were having a conversation so I left."

He started to laugh. Only his wife could see that Pancho was holding up his end of the discussion just fine.

"Anyway, I know you've been having trouble with flies. All the horses have. And I can't believe that all those chemicals in the repellents are good for them. So, according to this woman, if we put three drops of either lemongrass or citronella on Pancho's brush before you brush him down, the flies won't bother him."

Chance was silent, considering.

"I know how much Pancho would enjoy a fly-free day on the range. I know I would."

"You think it would work?"

"I thought the cows seemed happier."

"I didn't notice a difference."

"Chance, you didn't notice a difference because you haven't had the chance to observe them like I have. I'd like you to take a look at this book, because I think there are some pretty valid ideas for the ranch. I'd like to try them out. Sort of wean ourselves off as many chemicals as possible."

They were in agreement there.

"Okay. Tomorrow morning, you come down to the barn with me while I saddle up Pancho, and we'll try out this fly repellant. And I'll be outside with him all day, so is that a fair-enough test?"

She looked up at him and smiled. "I'll defer to your judgment on the matter."

CHANCE SAT in the large bathtub, the hot water soothing his sore muscles, and almost laughed out loud at his recollections of the day. Well, those cowboys had found essential oils in the cattle barn to be nothing short of hilarious, but they hadn't been laughing when both he and Pancho went through a completely fly-free working day.

"How come they're not bothering you?" If he'd had a nickel for every time he'd been asked that question, he'd be a rich man.

He sighed as he sank deeper into the water, and wondered where Cyn was. Eunice had told him she'd driven into town on the pretext of some errand or other. He knew she'd be back soon, but he'd missed having her at the ranch house when he came back.

What was it that Clark Gable had once said? *The most important thing a man can know is that as he approaches his own door, someone on the other side is listening for the sound of his footsteps.* And the only reason Chance remembered that quote was that Eunice had clipped it out of the paper and attached it to the front of the refrigerator with a magnet during the days when she'd despaired of his ever finding a wife and starting a family.

Well, his friend and housekeeper was happy now. She was crazy about Cyn, and ecstatic at the thought of the coming baby and how that child was going to liven things up at the ranch.

He heard the bedroom door slam shut, then steps approaching the bathroom. Cyn came in, then closed the toilet lid and sat down. She could barely contain her excitement.

"Well? How did the experiment go?"

He loved to tease her. Now he took his time wringing out a washcloth and wiping his face with it before he answered.

"Not a fly in sight."

"I knew it!" She bounced up and gave him a hug, then a kiss, then sat down on the rug next to the big claw-foot bathtub.

"Cyn?"

"Yes?"

"Can I ask you for a favor?"

"Anything."

"No pyramids over the bullpen, okay?"

She laughed. "Okay."

"And no crystals in the pigpen."

"I hear, master, and I obey. Chance, I'll tell you before I try anything else, that's a promise."

"It's just that I have my reputation as a traditional man to uphold. We have to ease the others on the ranch into change in a considerate way."

"I understand. Was Pancho happy with the experiment?"

"He sends you his thanks."

She kissed him. "I bought you a present," she whispered.

"Yes?"

"I called and asked Deva to Fed Ex me some base oils so I could make us a really good massage oil."

This caught his attention in a big way.

"Now, eucalyptus, peppermint and ginger would be excellent for sore muscles, so that's what I'll use for an oil for after work—"

"What about—what about a massage oil for those times when we just want to fool around?"

"I'm way ahead of you, cowboy. How does ylang-ylang sound to you?"

"Fine-fine."

She laughed. "There are a lot of oils recommended for sensual massages."

"And I'm sure we're going to work our way through all of them." He reached for her hand and grabbed it, entwining their fingers tightly as he pulled her toward the tub.

"Chance! I still have my clothes on!"

She fell into the tub with him and started to laugh as the water sloshed over the side.

"Not for long," he whispered between kisses. "Not for long."

Chapter Ten

"I think we should have a party," Cyn announced.

"Now, that's a good idea!" said Cookie.

They were seated around the kitchen table enjoying another of Eunice's breakfasts. Waffles with either heated maple syrup or peach preserves, homemade sausage and biscuits.

"What kind of a party?" Chance asked. He was so used to Cyn's ideas at this point that he just went with the flow.

"Well, the way I see it is that the ranch is sort of like a corporation."

"I agree with Cyn," Mark chimed in. Chance's cousin had become a regular a few times a week at breakfast. Cyn had found out that his wife, Debra, was as lousy a cook as she was which helped take a little of the sting out of that particular inadequacy.

Mark and Chance looked enough alike that Cyn found it intriguing. Now she watched as the two men considered her thoughts.

"And corporations give their employees certain perks. We can't offer anyone Lakers tickets or anything like that, but with the satellite dish and the wide-screen TV, we can offer the next best thing—"

"—An afternoon of football," Mark breathed, his tone touched with reverence. "That's right, you can get just about any game in the country!"

"We could cook up a bunch of food," Cyn began, then saw the four anxious faces turned in her direction. "Okay," she amended, "I'll help Eunice with the shopping and menu planning, but I'll leave the cooking up to her."

They all looked relieved. Even Bruce, who was lying beneath the table hoping a piece of sausage might accidently fall his way.

"What do you think?" She directed this question at her husband. "It would be a way of saying you appreciate all the hard work everyone's been up to, and kind of easing people into the colder weather, as well."

It was getting colder. Fall had arrived in all her glory, tinting the leaves with vivid color and making the mountains look even more striking in contrast. Cyn had pulled out her heavy sweaters, and never went anywhere without her coat and boots in the car.

Chance had been quite thorough in his explanation of the brutality of Wyoming's weather. Temperatures could change suddenly, blizzards could blow up, the weather could fluctuate in a heartbeat. A rancher always had to be prepared.

"I think it's a damn good idea," Chance said, rising from the table and grabbing his hat, then shrugging into his jacket. "I'll get word to the men as soon as you give me the date."

"This Sunday," Cyn replied.

"After church," Eunice added.

"Sounds good," said Mark.

"You stay out of that kitchen," Cookie said, and Cyn took his friendly teasing in stride. "You almost gave us all heart attacks with those oils, so we don't want any more tomfoolery."

"Cross my heart," she promised, then watched as the three men made their way from the kitchen door toward the barn and corrals.

"You still miss him when he leaves in the morning, don't you," Eunice said, her eyes bright.

"Every day. And even though I know he's going to be back at night, I—I just miss having him around."

"Uh-huh." Eunice was busy pulling out bowls and cups, measuring spoons and flour. Today was her day for baking, and the sooner she got to it, the better. "Well, that's the best there is in life, feeling that way about a man. You enjoy it."

Cyn knew what the older woman meant. Eunice had lost her husband a few years back, and from everything the housekeeper had told her, theirs had been a close and loving relationship. Life went on, Eunice said, but it was never quite the same.

"What can I help you with?" Cyn asked.

She admired Eunice for not quite giving in to the looks of fear the others had displayed when the mention of her presence anywhere near a kitchen had come up.

"You just sit at that table and tell me what Doc MacKay said about the baby on your last visit. Then, when you're done with that, you can tell me all about what you've been reading."

Eunice had proved to have an insatiable curiosity concerning the New Age books Deva had sent her. Now, conversations in the kitchen were just as likely to revolve around Chinese herbal healing as they were about bread baking.

"Okay. But first I'm going to take a little walk. The doctor was pretty adamant about my getting enough exercise. I don't want to blow up like a balloon."

"Take Bruce with you, he's restless."

Cyn stepped outside into the brisk fall wind and carefully closed the kitchen door behind her and Bruce. She'd tied her hair back this morning, and almost instantly wished she'd thought of a scarf. Her ears were cold. She snapped her fingers to get Bruce's attention, then began her brisk, daily walk.

This time she wandered toward the barn and past the bunkhouse. She was about to head back when she heard Cookie's distinctive voice from inside the structure.

"So's next Sunday, I want you all on your best behavior. We'll have a good old time, right?"

Cyn snapped her fingers for Bruce to follow her, then snuck closer to the window. It wouldn't hurt to hear how her husband's employees felt about the party.

"She won't be cooking, will she?" a voice asked.

"No." Cyn could hear the exasperation in Cookie's voice in that one-word answer. She took it in stride. Hell, she was a terrible cook and knew it.

"She's a strange one, ain't she?" another voice remarked. "Can't figure out why he up and married her when he had Doc Danvers right here in town so sweet on him."

Cyn stopped walking. Everything inside her stilled. She couldn't have moved away if her life depended on it.

"It ain't your business to figure it out," Cookie growled. "All I've got to know is how many of you will be up at the house this weekend."

"Yeah, but Cookie, you see what I'm getting at, don't ya? Rosie would've made him a better wife. She wouldn't be doing all those experiments with those oils—"

General laughter greeted that remark.

"—And getting up on the roof and changing everything all around—"

The laughter increased.

"Hell, the word in town's he had to marry her 'cause she up and got herself pregnant—"

"That's enough." Cookie's voice cut like a whip, but Cyn didn't stay around to hear any more. She stumbled away, her fingers entwined in Bruce's rolled leather collar, and let the Labrador lead her back toward the ranch house.

She'd never considered the fact that, to the townspeople or the cowboys who worked the C & M, she might seem like more of a liability to Chance than an

asset. Here she'd been so very foolish, trying her best
to be a good rancher's wife, and most of the men
thought her attempts were laughable. Pathetic.

She felt so foolish, because deep inside, she'd
thought she was doing a good job. What was it that
Chance had said that day in the bathtub? *We have to
ease the others on the ranch into change in a considerate way.*

He'd been trying, in his own way, to protect her from
their derision.

Did he feel the same way? Even a little?

Her heart was pounding so fast she felt sick. Tears
came to her eyes that had nothing to do with the sharp,
cutting wind. She let herself into the warmth of the
kitchen and thought about simply sitting down at the
kitchen table and having a good cry. She could tell
Eunice everything, and feel better.

No. She couldn't do that. She was already enough of
an oddity. She'd never let anyone, not even Chance,
know what she'd overheard this morning. And though
she wasn't sure if the cowboys on the ranch would ever
come to like her, she was damn well sure she was going
to win their respect.

But first, she had to know what Chance had passed
up because of his honorable way of looking at the
world. Had he had something going with Dr. Danvers, the town veterinarian? Had they had some sort of
unspoken agreement? And had she blundered into
Chance's life and wrecked their arrangement?

After all, sexual compatibility could only take you
so far. All the books and magazine articles stressed that

a couple had to have common interests, had to meet on a common ground. What could've been better than a rancher and a veterinarian? It sounded like a television series, like "The Waltons."

The kitchen smelled of cinnamon and sugar, of nutmeg and peeled oranges. Eunice was humming happily as she worked, and looked up in astonishment as Cyn came into the room.

"Do you think I'm stupid because I can't cook?"

Eunice's amazement was plain on her face. "What? Of course not! My mother couldn't cook to save her life, but she was one of the smartest women I ever met."

"Well, then, tell me what it is that I do."

Eunice stepped away from the counter and wiped her hands on her apron. "Honey, are you upset with me? Do you think I'm taking over what should be yours?"

"No. No, that's not the way I feel."

"All right. I want you to sit down and I'll make you some hot chocolate, and then—"

"Eunice, do you think I'm strange?"

She saw the sudden compassion in those hazel eyes, and knew with utter certainty that Eunice was aware of how she was perceived on the ranch. When the older woman spoke, her voice was very soft.

"Don't let a few damn fools poison the well. Do you understand what I'm saying?"

"I was pregnant when he married me."

There was a moment of silence in the kitchen, broken only by Bruce's nervous tail wagging, slapping against the kitchen floor.

"If that's supposed to make me feel less for the two of you, it isn't working."

"Maybe he could've done better."

"I don't think so."

Tears welled in her eyes, but she refused to let them fall. "Maybe he married me because he felt sorry for me."

"If you think that, you don't know that boy as well as you think you do."

"Maybe I don't know anything anymore."

"He loves you, Cyn. He never would have married you if he didn't. And you make him happy. He was a lonely man before you came into his life. You're both lucky enough to have a child on the way, and I'm not going to stand here and watch you work yourself up into a state and try to throw it all away."

"I don't know that I can believe that right now."

"Well, I want you to try."

"I'm going to go into town. Do you need anything?"

Eunice looked concerned. "What for?"

"I thought I might get Bruce some of that special diet food at the vet's. He's getting a little fat." She took the phone book, opened it up on the kitchen table and paged through it until she came to Rose Danvers, Veterinarian. She wrote the address down and stuffed the piece of paper in her pocket.

Eunice studied her, and Cyn deliberately kept her facial expression as bland as possible. She couldn't let Eunice know that she'd discovered who Chance had really wanted to marry.

"Would you check at the fabric store and see if the yarn I ordered has arrived?"

"Will do. Come on Bruce, let's go."

SHE DROVE CAREFULLY. As upset as she was, she wasn't going to get herself killed. After all, if she discovered Chance was still in love with this woman, they could always get divorced.

That shook her up enough that she had to pull off to the side of the road and stop the truck. Bruce whined and put his head in her lap, and she absently stroked his head as she finally let the tears fall.

"It never works for me," she told the dog in the quiet, warm confines of the truck cab. "Oh, I know I sound like I'm whining, but I don't understand. All I ever really wanted was a family, but it looks like—"

She couldn't finish the sentence, her throat hurt too much. So she sat in the truck, patting Bruce with one hand and resting the other over the gentle rounding of her stomach.

Chance would love their child, she was sure of that. But had he married her for the right reasons, or simply out of duty? He was working so hard to make the C & M a ranch he could be proud of, a ranch that would succeed. Did he need a wife who was nothing but a hindrance?

She composed herself and drove into town. Eunice's yarn hadn't arrived, so she snapped on Bruce's leash and walked down the street until she came to the veterinarian's office.

She couldn't go in.

Now, faced with the enormity of actually meeting the woman Chance had once supposedly loved, she couldn't do it. As she walked down the street, she wondered what had possessed her to come tearing into town on this errand, anyway.

She'd tell Eunice they'd been out of the diet food.

She and Bruce got into the truck, then headed back toward the ranch. They were driving along behind another car when a black-and-tan blur burst out of the bushes and sped directly in the path of the car in front of them.

The driver blasted his horn, then Cyn watched in horror as the car hit the small dog, didn't even stop, and drove away down the road.

She was shaking so badly she could barely pull the truck off the road, but she managed it. Leaving Bruce in the cab, she raced down the side of the road to where the badly injured animal was struggling to stand.

"Don't move," she called.

That did no good, as the dog saw her and attempted to run away. Cyn turned, ran back to the truck and grabbed the jacket Chance had made sure she always brought with her. Working carefully, she gathered the struggling animal into her arms and carried her back to the truck.

Bruce, bless him, was as calm and reliable as ever. He jumped into the truckbed while she settled the little stray into the seat beside her.

Back in town, she didn't even hesitate. She pulled the truck up in front of the vet's, then carried the dog inside the building.

The receptionist took one look at the animal's condition and ushered her inside one of the examining rooms.

Dr. Danvers was everything Cyn wasn't: petite, feminine, highly intelligent, competent—but Cyn didn't even care. All she wanted to know was what was going to happen to the dog.

"She's got a couple of broken ribs, and that leg doesn't look too good."

"I don't care. Do whatever you have to do. I'll wait here."

Cyn remained in the front room with Bruce, all the while wondering how another human being could hit a little dog with a car and keep driving. She forgot all about the diet food as she waited for the results of the surgery.

Afterward, Dr. Danvers came into the waiting room and Cyn stood up.

"She's a lucky little dog," the vet began.

Cyn couldn't control the tears that finally ran down her face. The dog would have a chance, after all. She swiped at them with her fingers as she reached for her checkbook.

"She's not your pet, is she?"

"She is now."

Rose Danvers smiled. "I'm always impressed by someone who helps a stray. There's no charge."

Cyn hadn't wanted to like her, but she did. This woman was perfect, an angel of mercy, and far more worthy of a man like Chance than she was. Rose Danvers had dark brown, wavy hair, blue eyes and a smattering of freckles across her finely boned face. She looked kind and gentle.

A perfect rancher's wife. And she'd bet her last dollar that she was at least a competent cook.

Cyn brought her mind back to the matter at hand. "Let me pay part of it, then."

"No, really. It's office policy."

Cyn knew when she was defeated. Well, at least by the time the baby was born and she left the C & M, Bruce could be well on his way to a svelte new doggy figure.

"I do need to buy some diet dog food. And some regular stuff, too, since she'll be going home with me."

"Is that Bruce?" Rose snapped her fingers and Bruce came galumphing up, bestowing wet, doggy kisses all over her fingers.

"Yep. He's getting to be quite a tub."

Rose laughed. "I've told Chance he should put him on a diet—" She stopped, and the air between the two women was charged with unspoken emotion.

The vet finally broke the silence. "You must be Chance's new wife. I'm Rose Danvers." She held out her hand.

Cyn couldn't quite understand it, but it seemed to her that Dr. Danvers had an air of defeat. Why would that happen, if Chance would've clearly been happier—

She took the offered hand and shook it. "Cyn Devereux." In a fit of sentimentality—and while under the influence of hypnosis—she'd taken Chance's last name, and was suddenly glad she'd made that decision.

"The whole town's been talking about you."

"I'll bet they have." Her voice was flat.

Rose gave her a look, as if she didn't quite know how to respond to that. "Well, let's weigh Bruce and get him started on his diet."

BY THE TIME SHE HEADED toward home, it was late in the afternoon. Bruce, exhausted by even the thought of a diet, lay quietly sleeping in the seat beside her. The stray would be staying at the vets for the next few days until she was well enough to come back to the ranch.

Cyn was so tired she didn't know what to think. She simply drove the truck up in front of the ranch house, let Bruce out and watched as the black Labrador loped onto the front porch, then around back toward the doggy door near the kitchen. She sat behind the wheel, staring straight ahead.

What had that therapist once said, about both her and Pepper having overactive imaginations? She didn't know what to do or how to feel about her predicament. All she knew was that she had to get off her feet. Climbing into bed and pulling the covers over her head sounded like the best idea she'd had in a long time.

Far better than the stupid party.

The sooner this horrible day came to an end, the better.

She let herself in the front door, avoiding the kitchen and Eunice's knowing eyes. If anyone saw the truck out front, they'd know she was home. She climbed up the stairs and was almost to the master bedroom when Chance opened the door and stepped out into the hall.

The look on his face shocked her, then she realized how she had to look, her hair blown all over, the jacket covered with blood. Before she had time to think, he'd gathered her into his arms and was carrying her into the bedroom.

He eased the jacket off her shoulders, then pulled her into his arms and held her tightly.

"I'm okay," she whispered. "I just saw an accident—"

"Rosie called. She thought you looked pale when you left and she was concerned. Eunice took the call, then asked Cookie to come get me. I was just about to leave and come look for you—"

"Oh, Chance. I didn't want to interrupt your day—"

"Don't think that way. I'm not angry with you, I was worried—"

"All I do is cause trouble—"

"That's not true." He held her more tightly in his arms and began to gently rock her, and the love that she felt coming from him was so overwhelming that she burst into tears and sobbed into his shirtfront.

She didn't want to lose this man. Not ever. She wanted to spend the rest of her life with him, raise their children together. She wanted him to be proud of her, to be happy with his decision to marry her—

And right about now, all of those goals seemed about as attainable as flying to the moon.

He helped her undress, then tucked her into bed. He brought up a bowl of Eunice's homemade soup, then sat with her while she ate it. Then he told her he had just a few more chores he had to attend to, and he would be back with her shortly.

"I'm just going to sleep, Chance. Don't hurry on my account."

"I'll come home to you as soon as I can."

When she woke later that evening, he was in their bed beside her, fast asleep, his arms warm and strong around her. She moved into his warmth and felt his grip on her tighten. He looked so tired that she was glad he slept, and she merely kissed him on the cheek before she snuggled close and fell back asleep, feeling safer than she had in a long time.

THE PARTY was a smashing success.

But only because Cyn prepared for it with the same sort of tactical skill a military general brought to a major battle.

A good night's sleep put everything in perspective. So what if a couple of cowboys thought she wasn't the greatest wife Chance could have picked—he'd picked her, hadn't he? And that was what counted.

She couldn't cook, she wasn't what anyone would call sensible by the slightest stretch of the imagination, and she wasn't the ideal candidate for a rancher's wife. But if love for her husband counted for anything, she had plenty to spare. She knew nothing about ranch life, but was willing to learn. She'd become fascinated with New Age remedies and philosphies, and if those men didn't agree with her way of approaching things, that was just plain tough.

She was, if nothing else, a survivor.

And she would survive this.

The first call she made, as soon as she woke up, was to the vet's to see how her stray was doing. The receptionist assured her that the little dog was coming along just fine. The next call she put in was to her girlfriend Abby, in Las Vegas. Abby had been in Europe shopping for her boutique during the entire week Chance had blown in, or she would have insisted on meeting him. As it was, she begged to be allowed to come visit sometime after the holidays, and Cyn agreed.

"You can help me with the baby," she teased. Abby was pure glamour, and the thought of her friend changing a diaper or dealing with what the little darlings spit up brought a smile to her face.

"Don't laugh, I love kids. I want some of my own, someday," Abby said, surprising her.

"Have you seen Pepper?"

"I have, and I told her she was acting abominably toward you."

Trust Abby not to mince words.

"Well, my darling, what do you want?"

When Cyn explained her predicament, Abby roared with laughter. "I love a project like this one! I'll go through every dress in my boutique, pick out three or four, and send them to you ASAP."

"You are a godsend."

The dresses arrived within days. Cyn had described her figure problems to Abby—a great bustline and a growing tummy. Abby had sent her several dresses that accentuated the positive and concealed the negative, along with some stunning French underwear, up-to-the-minute makeup and killer perfume.

Before the party, she'd requested total privacy, even from Chance. He'd been amused, but indulged her. Cyn had spent almost four hours getting ready, pulling out all the stops. The dresses Abby had sent her were deceptively glamorous. Casual, but elegant. Any of them would have worked, but the one she finally selected was a brilliant piece of designing magic.

She gave herself a manicure, a pedicure and actually set her hair. She took a ton of time with her makeup, and then spritzed herself with Abby's heavenly perfume.

When she walked into that room full of cowboys, you could've heard those jaws drop 'round the world.

"Hi. It's so nice to finally meet you all."

She circulated. She mingled. She smiled until she thought her face would crack. She listened to voices carefully until she found the ones she'd heard that afternoon—and she killed those bastards with kindness.

"Another drink?"

"More dip?"

"Oh, try the quesadillas, they're fabulous! Eunice is so talented in the kitchen, I admire her so much. Me? I look at a stove and it breaks."

She appropriated Marilyn Monroe's kittenish, playful approach to men mixed with Sharon Stone's killer intelligence. She set her goals out clearly and fought to attain them.

Take no prisoners.

Show no mercy.

Survive and prosper.

And through it all, she felt Chance's eyes on her. He knew exactly what she was up to, and his facial expression clearly conveyed his amusement. And admiration.

By the time she was done working that room, every cowboy in the place was a candidate for helping her understand how a ranch was run. They were a groveling mess of masculinity, sprawled at her stiletto-heeled feet.

She played the dumb blonde—in this case, redhead—to the hilt.

"You mean you actually go out and do all that in a single day? Aren't you clever!"

She killed them with kindness. She stroked that proverbial male ego until it was inflated to gigantic proportions. She teased and flirted and made each man in the room feel she was focused solely on him and his achievements.

The chili was hot, the beer ice cold, and the chocolate cake served at halftime a masterpiece of the culinary arts. But the true work of art was Cyn's performance.

She wasn't going to let any of those men leave her home thinking she was anything less than the perfect companion for Chance.

The party lasted until the wee hours of the morning, even though Chance warned everyone that they would still be expected to get up before sunrise as usual the following day. Cyn stood at the front door with her husband as the last few ranch hands straggled into the night toward the bunkhouse. She personally said goodbye to each of the men, waving her hand playfully.

"Pull that hat on, Clyde, it's cold out. I'll get that fly repellant oil for Buster to you in the morning."

"Take care of that leg, Bob. I'll have Cookie bring you a soothing muscle rub tomorrow."

"Sam, I don't like the sound of that cough. Maybe you could stop by tomorrow for dinner and some of Eunice's French onion soup."

She couldn't contain her triumph as she headed up the stairs, Chance right behind her. They'd barely shut the door to their bedroom before he was working on the fastenings to her dress.

"Do you do this all deliberately, or are you truly unconscious in your attempts to drive me crazy?"

"Whatever are you talking about?" But she couldn't repress her laughter.

The dress was off and he set to work on the fastenings of the plunge-front, push-up bra. He hadn't missed the garter belt and stockings, either.

"I'm talking about the performance you gave in the family room tonight."

She concentrated on unfastening his pants and did a little sensual exploring of her own.

He groaned, and all conversation came to a dead halt as he kissed her, then maneuvered her toward the bed. They sprawled across it, and he wasn't concerned with getting any more of her clothing off. He simply stripped off his own and slid between her thighs, a smile on his face.

"You," he whispered, "are quite a turn-on."

"Chance," she said mock-seriously. "You'll have to be up before sunrise—"

"I'm up now—"

"You know what I mean. It's not good to burn the candle at both ends, and—ahhh!"

He sank inside her, and she dug her nails into his back.

"Chance," she whispered.

He didn't say anything, he merely kissed her mouth, her neck, her breasts.

And afterward, when they lay entwined on their bed, clothes flung all around, she whispered, "Do you like being married to me?"

"What are you, crazy? If I liked it any more than I do now, I'd have a coronary."

She laughed, and fell asleep in his arms.

Chapter Eleven

Chance accompanied her to her doctor's appointment in early November. Winter had struck with full force, and he told her in no uncertain terms that he didn't want her out on the roads alone. As Cyn felt she was about as graceful and elegant as one of the hippos in *Fantasia,* she acquiesced to his wishes. And she was grateful, because she knew what it cost him, to take a long afternoon away from the never-ending work on the ranch.

"How'd it go?" he asked as she came out of the examining room.

"Your wife," Dr. MacKay said, a smile on his portly face, "is as healthy as the proverbial horse."

"And as big as one, too," Cyn muttered.

Chance gave her a hug and a kiss. "Not to me."

"Then you've got to be blind." She couldn't believe how much weight she'd gained since her last visit. Her due date was technically right around Christmas, but the doctor had warned her that first babies usually arrive a little late.

"You take care of yourself," the doctor called after her as Chance opened the door for her.

She waved back, then braced herself for the onslaught of frigid air. It had never been this cold in Las Vegas, and she was still adjusting to the brutality of a Wyoming winter. Now, as she followed Chance down the sidewalk in town—using him as a windbreak—she wondered at how she had to look, all roly-poly and wrapped up in her bulky winter coat.

"How about a piece of pie at Thelma's before we head on out?" Chance asked.

She'd rather die than add any more calories to this frame, but she wanted to be agreeable. So she smiled and said "sure" and they headed toward the one coffee shop in town.

Thelma herself greeted Chance like a long-lost son, but gave Cyn a rather reserved smile as she showed them to a corner booth. Cyn couldn't blame her. She'd been in only twice before, and it took a little time for the natives to warm up to a stranger. She wasn't concerned. One thing she had was plenty of time.

Over the past few weeks she'd come to the conclusion that Chance was a happy man. She'd even relaxed a bit and decided that perhaps she could hope for a little happiness for herself. She'd actually finished the baby afghan, and it looked halfway decent up in the nursery, along with a crib, a dresser, a changing table and an enormous amount of toys. Everything was ready for its tiny occupant to arrive.

She still missed her twin tremendously, and had written Pepper several long letters. She'd been careful not to make any reference to the baby, only to the ranch, describing a typical day, telling her about Eunice and Cookie, Bruce and Lucky—the stray—and expressing the hope that her sister and husband could come visit them soon.

She'd received no answer. Yet. But she still allowed herself to hope.

Now Thanksgiving was just around the corner, and Christmas mere weeks away. Soon, she'd hold her baby in her arms, the baby she and Chance had created.

Often, late at night, Cyn would lie awake in bed and wonder at the way fate had truly thrown the two of them together. Then she would pray, in her own way, and offer up a silent thank you. She loved Chance so deeply, and couldn't imagine a better life than working with him on the ranch and raising their children.

She'd never felt herself to be more of a partner than she did with Chance. Before, she'd always been the leader, the strong one. Now she felt that she and Chance were in this together, working toward a common goal. There was no job in the outside world that could offer her the deep satisfaction she felt while working and living on the ranch.

And she'd assured Chance, over and over, that she never had a chance to even think about being bored. She had so many interests, she loved the animals and living close to nature. Each day was different, and a gift.

She'd come to love this wild Western part of the world, and liked the Code of the West she saw in action almost every day. Doing what was right, helping your neighbor and keeping your word. It was a simpler way of life, and she responded to it wholeheartedly. Her husband had been raised among these people, and she was coming to understand what had shaped him into the man he was.

She knew he loved ranching, that it almost defined him. Chance loved not being a part of the rat race, not having to fight traffic in a daily commute, and not having to participate in office politics or other games in the workplace. He'd told her once that he loved the feeling of actually seeing what it was he accomplished every day.

Now, his workdays were longer than ever. Working a ranch was an investment of emotion, time and hard work. The effect of the brutal winter weather on the cattle was crucial. They had to be fed every day, and she learned that Chance would put out more hay than they could all eat rather than shortchange a single animal.

She came to see that the animals were more than a source of profit to Chance. He thought of himself as their protector, and he wouldn't let them down. She loved him for it, for it was that same impulse that had led her to rescue the little mixed breed dog from the side of the road.

Chance never seemed to complain, though his workload didn't lessen as the winter progressed. There were waterholes that had to be chopped, as the cattle couldn't break the ice themselves. And there were always the sick ones that had to be doctored.

The more time Cyn spent observing her husband and listening to how he spent his workday, the more she grew to love and respect him. And to have a quiet type of faith in him.

She was changing, for Chance was the first person in her entire life she'd ever come to depend on. There was still a small part of her she held in reserve, probably in self-defense. But she was growing to depend on him more and more, especially as her pregnancy advanced and she came to feel so helpless and vulnerable.

"What kind of pie do you want?" Chance asked, breaking into her thoughts.

She wondered what he would say if she told him exactly what she'd been thinking. "Banana cream."

"That sounds good. Coffee?"

"Nope. I'll have another disgusting glass of milk."

He laughed and set down his menu.

Their order had just arrived when Cyn glanced up and saw Rose come in the front door of the coffee shop. She stood there for a second, probably enjoying the warmth, then headed toward the counter. As it was late in the afternoon, Cyn guessed she was probably stopping by for dinner on her way home.

It struck her, then, that Rose had probably dreamed of sitting down to dinner with Chance every night. But now that dream was impossible. A rush of compassion filled her, and she remembered how she'd hated eating alone. Hated it so much her refrigerator had contained only a wilted head of lettuce and a few beers.

"Chance," she whispered.

He glanced up at her, having been preoccupied with his coffee and pie.

"There's Rose."

He glanced in her direction, but Cyn could see no change of emotion in his expression. Whatever her husband thought about what had once been between him and the town's vet, he hid his feelings well.

"I hate to see her eat alone. Why don't we ask her to join us?"

He got up and walked over toward the counter. Cyn watched as Rose caught sight of him, the way her facial expression and body language changed. And she knew with a woman's intuition that Rose Danvers was still in love with her husband, though she also sensed the woman would do nothing to threaten her marriage.

When Chance came back, he slid in beside her, giving Rose the other side of the booth to herself. They talked about ranching, and Rose told them of a few of the animals she'd treated that week. When her dinner came, conversation ceased for a short time, then she ordered dessert and asked a few questions about the baby, how they met, and wished them a very happy Thanksgiving.

Cyn knew how hard this had to be for her, and she gave the woman credit for having a lot of class.

On the way home, she decided to ask Chance how he felt about the whole thing. She got her courage up and blurted out her question before fear got the better of her.

"Do you ever regret marrying me?"

His surprise was genuine. "No. Why would you think that?"

"I mean . . . did you . . . do you ever think that Rose might have made a better rancher's wife?"

They were almost home, and he guided the truck carefully over the packed snow in the long driveway until they were safely parked in front of the ranch house. Then he turned to face her and took both her hands in his.

"No. I never thought that."

She studied his face in the early evening light, and wondered if he was trying to spare her feelings.

"Cyn." He took off his leather glove and stroked her cheek with his hand. "Rose and I grew up together, went to school together. I took her to the prom, and we thought we were in love that year. But if I'd wanted to marry her, I'd have married her. I wanted to marry you, so I married you."

Male logic. She could tell now that he'd told her this, he considered this particular discussion closed. Finished business. While she was still going round and round, analyzing all the emotional ramifications.

"She's—"

She's still in love with you.

She couldn't get the words out, for in a peculiar way she thought that saying them would be a betrayal of Rose Danvers. The woman had no reason to like her, yet had been nothing but kind to her. And she'd saved Lucky's life.

"She's—an awfully nice woman."

"I think so. Maybe in time, the two of you could be friends."

Men.

She followed him into the house, letting him shield her from the winter wind with his large body.

THANKSGIVING WAS ONE of the best holidays she could remember, except for the absence of her twin. And Cyn decided, feelings or no feelings, she was going to call her sister and talk to her.

Luca answered the phone and told her Pepper was sleeping.

"Did she get my letters?"

"Yes."

"Why won't she talk to me?"

"I don't know, Cyn. I tell her every day, you cannot treat your sister this way. Family is family, you know?"

"I know. Look, Luca, would you tell her to call me when she gets up. I don't care how late it is, I really want to talk to her. Okay?"

Her nerves were tightly strung through the remainder of the evening, and when the phone rang, she jumped.

"For you," Chance said, and she chose to take the call in the kitchen.

"Hi, Cyn, how are you?" Her twin's voice sounded thin and strained across the phone connection.

"Great. And you?"

"Oh, doing fine."

There were so many things she wanted to tell her, but she couldn't.

"How's Luca? Did he cook one of his spectacular dinners?" *The baby kicks a lot now, I can feel her move. Don't ask me why, but I'm sure I'm going to have a girl.*

"Yeah. We had Deva and Abby over for dinner. Abby has a new boyfriend."

"That's great. What did Luca make for dessert?" *I wish I could talk to you about all the conflicting emotions I've been feeling. Just to know you were still there for me would mean so much....*

"A pumpkin soufflé. What did you eat?"

"Eunice made the most incredible pies, I'll have to send you guys the recipes for the crusts." *Pepper, I love you, please talk to me.*

"Cyn...I'm sorry I haven't been much of a...sister to you."

Cyn didn't know what to say. She listened, and she could hear her heart pounding in her throat.

"I'm here, Pep. Please keep talking to me."

"I went and had...some tests."

She knew then. She knew, and the tears began to run down her face, hard and fast. One thing about being a twin, you had these feelings, you knew when something just wasn't right.

"Oh, Pepper."

"I can't...I can't..."

"I know." She didn't want her sister to have to hurt any more by even saying the words. I'm sorry seemed so inadequate when the loss was this enormous. Fate had been cruel this time around, denying Pepper the children she wanted so badly.

"Please don't . . ." Pepper was crying now, and Cyn heard her twin blowing her nose. "Please don't tell me about the joys of adopting, because I just don't want to hear it right now."

"Okay."

There was a short silence, then Pepper said, "Are you doing okay?"

Cyn wasn't sure she wanted to hear about the baby, so her reply was deliberately vague. "Oh, you know me, the doctor says I'm as healthy as a horse." She could've kicked herself as soon as the words were out of her mouth.

"Pep, I'm sorry—"

"No, it's okay." She heard her twin take a deep breath over the phone. "I'm making something for the nursery. It's a counted cross-stitch thing with teddy bears on it."

Now she had to blow her nose. "That means a lot to me."

"When are you due?"

"Right around Christmas. Pepper . . . I'd love for you and Luca to come visit and stay for a while, but I'll understand if you don't want to."

"No, I . . . I was thinking the other day that if . . . I can't be a . . . mother, then I can certainly be the world's greatest aunt."

"I know you will be."

"Have you thought of any names?"

"Nope." She had, of course, as had Chance, but she didn't want to prolong her twin's torment. Pepper had already gone above and beyond the call of what one sister did for another, considering the circumstances.

"I love you, Pep. I miss you."

"Me, too. Give that cowboy of yours a hug for me. Cyn, he's really handsome." She blew her nose again, and her tone brightened a little when she continued speaking. "I can't believe you kept him hidden from all us for such a long time."

"Yeah...me neither."

Afterward, she sat by the phone for almost ten minutes, thinking of the enormity of what her sister had lost. To want children so badly, to have wanted them for so long, and to be unable to have them...

She sat down at the kitchen table, put her head in her hands and started to sob.

Chance found her that way, and he simply pulled up a chair next to her, put his arm around her and let her cry. She told him about the call, and he listened, his dark blue eyes filled with pain.

"Would you have stayed with me if you found out I couldn't have children?" she asked on a hiccup of a sob, then started to laugh with reaction. "What a stupid question, we wouldn't even be together if I hadn't gotten pregnant."

He took one of her hands in his and studied it. His touch soothed her, and she felt her racing heart start to calm down.

"I would stay with you no matter what. And that's a promise. I love you, Cyn, and sometimes I think you just won't let yourself believe it."

"No, I do. I do." Another little piece of the wall she'd placed between herself and this man shattered.

CYN THREW HERSELF into the spirit of Christmas to take her mind off her sister's pain. She bought presents for everyone, wrapped them in elaborate paper, mailed everything early, put up a huge tree in the family room. Wreaths adorned all the doors on the ranch house, she created ridiculous bows for the dogs, and pine swags appeared mysteriously in the stables.

She baked cookies for the ranch hands—under Eunice's watchful eye—and discovered something she could make that turned out well at last. Why cookies, she'd never know, but at last she had a culinary accomplishment that didn't become a total disaster.

Now, with everything prepared for the holidays, food bought, menus planned, she sat back and did little last-minute things. Eunice taught her to knit, and Cyn decided at the last minute that she was going to make simple slippers for everyone on her Christmas list, including Chance.

"But I don't wear anything at all to bed," he insisted one night in their bedroom as they lay in bed, the snow tapping against the windows, the dogs curled up on the foot of the puffy comforter, everyone quite cozy and tucked in for the night.

"You'll wear these babies if I have to staple them to your feet," Cyn muttered as she ripped out another three rows of stitches. She was still having a little trouble reading patterns.

A soft knock at the door disturbed them, but Chance was out of bed in a flash, reaching for his red plaid robe, belting it securely around him before he opened the door.

Eunice stood there, a worried look in her eyes. She exchanged a few words with Chance, he nodded his head, then closed the door and headed for his closet.

"What happened?" Cyn put her knitting down and got out of bed.

He was already almost dressed. "Gracie's in trouble."

Gracie was one of the mares due to foal. Cookie slept out in the stable in a special room just off the stalls, and he'd been keeping an eye on the high-strung mare. Chance finished dressing, then reached for the phone. Cyn knew he'd dial Rose Danver's emergency number.

"Rosie? Chance. It's Gracie. Okay, I'll have one of the men meet you by the road. Thanks."

He hung up the phone, gave her a swift kiss, then started down the stairs.

Hampered by her extreme bulk, it took Cyn almost twenty minutes to get dressed. She made it down to the kitchen in time to find Eunice fixing thick sandwiches and a large thermos of black coffee.

"That poor man will be up all night, and if I know him he'll ride out in the morning to see to the cattle as if nothing at all happened," she muttered as she darted around her kitchen, getting the food ready for Cookie, Chance and Rose.

"I'll take it out to them."

"You will not. You'll stay right here and keep warm. Chance doesn't need to worry about you out there, getting cold and wet."

Cyn immediately saw Eunice's logic. "You're right, I'll stay here. Is there anything I can do to help you?"

"Get some of those cookies we made out of the jars and let's pack them in with the sandwiches. I have a feeling Gracie is going to give them a long night."

Within the hour, Rose arrived. She headed straight out to the stable. Eunice had just put on her coat and was wrapping a thick woolen scarf around her head when Sam, one of the ranch hands, appeared at the kitchen door, stamping snow off his boots.

"Now, don't you go out in this nasty weather, Eunice. I'll take that food to them."

"Bless you, Sam. I wasn't looking forward to it."

He smiled at her, his craggy face transformed. "I never forgot that soup, ma'am. It helped my cough."

"Good."

She and Cyn handed Sam the baskets of food, and he headed out into the night, toward the stable.

"What now?" Cyn asked, "I don't think I can get back to sleep, thinking about Gracie."

"I know I can't." Eunice sighed. "Poor little thing. Well, looks like we might as well put on a pot of coffee, get out some cookies and play some cards."

THE NIGHT PASSED so slowly, Cyn thought she would go out of her mind. Eunice finally nodded off in her chair by the old-fashioned stove, and Cyn stared out the window toward the light above the barn door.

What was taking them so long? Was Gracie going to be all right? She stared at the phone, willing Chance to call them from Cookie's office and tell them that everything was all right.

Silence. Not a sound except the tapping of snow against the windowpanes. Eunice slept soundly, and Cyn brought in one of the afghans from the family room and tucked it around the older woman, then turned off the low flame beneath the coffeepot on the stove.

She sat for a while, and said a silent prayer for the mare. Then, when she could stand it no longer, she threw on her coat and boots and let herself out into the cold, snowy night.

She reached the barn in short order, and as she knew where Gracie's stall was, she headed straight toward it. She saw lights, and a gathering of men. None of them noticed her as she slipped past them and looked inside the large stall.

The image she saw would stay with her the rest of her life.

There was a great deal of blood. Chance held the mare's head, talking soothingly with her as Rose worked frantically to ease the laboring mother's distress. It was clear from the stark grimness of both their expressions that something had gone terribly wrong, and they were fighting for Gracie's life.

She couldn't move. Her legs didn't seem to belong to her. She wasn't about to faint, but she couldn't seem to look away, and the longer she stared the more horrible the scene in front of her became.

Chance must have sensed her there because he looked up at the same moment he used a bloody hand to flick his hair off his face. She would remember the terrible expression in his blue eyes for as long as she lived, along with the bright red smear of blood along his forehead.

"Sam," he said quietly, his voice flat and devoid of any emotion at all. "Get her out of here. Now."

Sam took her arm and walked her all the way back to the ranch house, sat her down at the table and made her drink a cup of coffee with milk and sugar in it. They woke Eunice, and when Sam told her what had happened, the woman sprang into action.

"If anyone can save that mare, then Chance Devereux can. He raises cattle, but he's a genius with horses. Rose will do her best, and she's the best vet we've had in the county for a long time. So now the only thing we can do is pray for that little gal and hope she pulls through."

Cyn nodded her head, but she couldn't get the image of all the blood out of her mind. She could still smell it, the warm, metallic scent, and see the way drops of it had splashed on the walls of the stall. Chance's arms had been covered....

She closed her eyes and started to pray. For all of them, Chance, Rose, and especially Gracie and her unborn foal.

She was still awake and sitting in one of the chairs by the kitchen window when she saw Chance leaving the barn. Without thinking, she grabbed her coat and headed out the door, meeting him halfway on his walk to the ranch house. He staggered a little with exhaustion as she caught him around the waist, then leaned into her. She tried to give him all the strength she could, all the time hoping luck had been on their side.

The minute she saw his eyes, she knew.

"She just made it. Barely. But neither of them are out of the woods yet."

"What are you going to do?"

"Rose is with them now. She asked me to bring her back some more coffee and another sandwich."

"I can do that."

And she did. All cooking jokes aside, she knew how to make a pot of coffee, and sandwiches were something a child could make. Eunice had fallen back asleep in her chair, and Cyn didn't want to wake her for something as simple as this. As she wrapped the sandwiches in foil, she felt Chance's strong hands settle on her shoulders.

"Don't be scared by what you saw."

"I'm not," she lied, not wanting to add to his burdens. "Remember what Doc MacKay said, I'm as healthy as a—" She stopped, remembering the animal he'd compared her to.

"Chance, I'm fine."

"Good girl. Now I want you to go upstairs, get some sleep, and take care of that baby. Will you do that for me?"

She nodded her head.

"Good."

She gave him a quick kiss, hating to see him so exhausted but knowing he wouldn't sleep until Gracie and her foal had a better chance of surviving. Chance had a deep feeling for all the animals on his ranch, he considered himself to be their protector, and he wouldn't let Gracie down now.

She watched him walk to the barn, watched him until he disappeared inside the door and she couldn't see him anymore.

"You married a damn good man," Eunice said from the depths of the afghan.

"I know."

The older woman smiled. "It does my heart good to see the two of you helping each other."

Briefly, Cyn told her about her visit to Gracie's stall and what she saw.

"He didn't want you to see that, not with your time so near. That's why he wanted you to stay in the kitchen."

"I didn't think. I just wanted to see how she was. How he was."

"Don't think about it now, honey. Go on upstairs and get some rest."

She did, but she couldn't sleep. Cyn simply lay in bed and waited until she heard familiar footsteps coming up the stairs. She almost laughed at the picture she and the two dogs made on the large bed, all alert for Chance's return.

He came inside and kicked off his boots, then fell on the bed with all his clothes on. He gave her a quick kiss and was asleep almost as soon as his head hit the pillow.

She watched him and a great wave of tenderness engulfed her. Slowly, gently, as carefully as she could, she undressed him and tucked him beneath the covers. Then she closed the curtains against the sunlight already pouring in the windows.

Once Chance was comfortably in bed, she snuck down into the kitchen, where Eunice assured her that the men would take on Chance's chores for the day. All the cattle would be fed, everything that needed to get done would get done.

She went back upstairs then and watched him sleep. She wanted to be there when he woke up, so Cyn snuggled back down beneath the covers, nudged both Bruce and Lucky around so there was a little more room in their bed, and closed her eyes.

Just before she fell asleep, she said another silent little thank you and sent up one last silent prayer because Gracie and her foal had been spared. She knew Chance would've been devastated had anything happened to either animal. As she slipped into an exhausted slumber she realized that this was part of what truly loving a man meant, that sometimes you felt his feelings more deeply than your own.

Chapter Twelve

Christmas was magical.

She'd never realized what it was she'd truly missed until she experienced Christmas at the C & M Ranch. It snowed the night before, and as Cyn looked out the bedroom window that morning, she saw a vast vista of white, the trees thickly coated with snow, the sky a leaden grey. There were still clouds in the sky, and she knew they were in for more rough weather.

Chance teased her by pretending to sleep on, but even he couldn't keep up the act when Lucky started to lick his face. He laughed, opened his eyes, swung his legs over the side of the bed, stretched and began his day.

They opened their presents after all the animals were taken care of. But before that, Eunice outdid herself with a spectacular breakfast. A *strata* with eggs, cheese, ham and broccoli. Cinnamon rolls and various muffins. Fruit compote, a mimosa punch, and her pan-fried breakfast potatoes.

And the cookies. Both she and Cyn had outdone themselves. Of course, sugar cookies and spice cookies. But also plates of jam thumbprints, butterhorns, candy cane cookies, cranberry orange cookies and *pepparkakor*. Eunice's mother had been of Norwegian descent, and had taught her to make the thin, spicy Christmas cookie.

While Finns traditionally cut out pigs and Swedes cut out goats, Cyn had found a cooking catalog and ordered cookie cutters in the shape of cattle, horses and cowboy boots. She'd even had a C & M cookie cutter specially made.

The look on Chance's face when he'd seen that had been worth the difficulty she'd had keeping the secret.

Some of the ranch hands had family in the area, and they went off to visit them. Others were alone in the world, drifters who had come to settle at the C & M. Cyn took them plates of cookies, and she and Eunice arranged for a ham and a turkey to be brought over to the bunkhouse, along with several side dishes and various drinks. The celebration inside the ranch house would only include Chance and Cyn, Eunice, Cookie and Sam.

Cyn was enchanted with the way the older cowboy kept giving their housekeeper very special looks. Eunice pretended not to notice, but Cyn could tell she was pleased.

Some romances started because of hypnosis, but Eunice would look back and probably decide that this particular romance had been cemented over a bowl of hot soup.

After breakfast, they all moved to the redecorated family room, carrying plates of cookies and mugs of hot cocoa. Cyn had gone wild buying CDs with Christmas music, and now the sweet sound of Amy Grant singing Christmas carols filled the large room.

It had been decorated to perfection, as had the nursery. She'd had time to throw a few more quilts on their bed, and mess with the master bedroom curtains, but any more decorating would have to wait until after the baby was born. She already had sketches in her notebook for what she planned to do to Chance's office, and she and Eunice had conferred about the kitchen.

But all that could wait for now.

She was nervous about what she'd bought her husband, and hoped he would like his gifts as much as she had. Packages were passed around, and wrapping paper was shredded and hit the floor.

Cyn held her breath.

She watched as Chance opened his first few presents. She'd bought him a few functional things, sweaters and socks and long underwear, because she couldn't bear the way he went out in the cold. She wanted him to feel protected and warm.

His first few gifts to her surprised her, as well. Flannel nightgowns and warm socks.

When he opened his hand-knit slippers, he laughed.

When she started on a huge package labeled as hers, she didn't know what to think. The wrapping fell away, and she found herself looking at a saddle.

She glanced up at Chance, and he looked like a little boy about to explode with pent-up excitement. He led her to the window, and she saw Ringo and Buddy standing in the snow. Between them was the most beautiful horse she'd ever seen. A palomino, with only a halter, stood between the two men, her pale mane ruffled by the winter wind.

Cyn's throat closed as she turned to her husband, and he must have read the incredulous expression on her face.

"For you." He answered her question before she voiced it. "Her name's Penny, and she's gentle as a kitten." He cleared his throat, then said, "I thought you might want to ride with me—after the baby's born."

She smiled up at him, then went into his arms, her cheek against his solid chest.

"You guessed exactly right. Can I go out and see her?"

"Ringo and Buddy will take her back to the stable. We can go out there in a little bit. I don't want you out in this cold."

"I'm pregnant, not incapacitated."

"You need a keeper." But he said it with a smile.

He was even more perceptive with another present. Cyn stared down at the boxed set of colored pencils and several sketch pads, then back up at her husband. He seemed very pleased with himself.

"Those sketches you did—the family room, the den. I thought they were really good. I thought you might—

want to see what you could do if you had the time to do some drawing."

In a heartbeat, she remembered the art classes she'd had as a little girl, in public school. She'd loved creating that way, but it had all been put aside because things had been so complicated. She'd never had time to pursue what had really mattered to her, things that fed her soul.

"Thank you, Chance."

She watched as he opened his other gifts. The boxed set of classical CDs was a great success, as Chance had a CD player in the truck he drove around the ranch and sometimes liked to listen to music. There were times, he told her, when the silence of the ranch was just fine. There were other times when he needed to hear music.

Books, videos and games later, he came to the one package that made Cyn hold her breath. As he tore away the bright wrapping paper, her heart sped up.

Then he smiled.

She'd had to do some fierce negotiating with the owner of The Branding Iron, but she'd managed to talk him out of one of the mirrors that had hung above the bar. It was a large mirror, with the bar's logo of a cowboy branding cattle etched into the reflective surface.

When he looked at her, she knew he was remembering.

"It was that," she whispered so the others wouldn't hear, "or a home hypnosis course."

"That could've been interesting."

"I'm sure."

"No, think about the possibilities. A whole slew of words that would make you jump to my bidding—"

As he set the large mirror carefully aside, she sat in his lap and gave him a quick kiss. "I already ensure that your slightest wish is my command."

His glance moved upward, in the general direction of their bedroom, then he whispered exactly what he wanted to do to her in her ear, causing her to blush furiously.

It was a Christmas she'd never forget.

THAT NIGHT, CHANCE WENT to the window of their bedroom and stared up into the night sky. Cyn was asleep in their bed behind him, securely tucked in against the winter cold.

He looked up at the sky and thought about many things, but chief among them he wondered if his wife would ever come to trust him.

Things were working between them. The marriage would be a success, he was certain of that. But there was still a part of her she held away from him, apart, protecting herself. What he wanted, more than anything, more than any present, was the sense that she trusted him. He wanted her to give over to him, to make that essential feminine step that was crucial to him.

He wanted to feel that she trusted him to protect her. He'd tried to show her, in countless ways, that she could lean on him, depend on him, rely on him. And he didn't know what else to do.

He knew most of her history. An alcoholic mother, a father who'd walked out before she and her twin were even born. He also knew some people were simply born stronger than others, both physically and mentally. Even spiritually. As a rancher, he saw it manifested all the time in the animals he protected.

Cyn had been stronger. She was a survivor. She'd never have made it through all she had if the fates had dealt her another kind of personality. Pepper wouldn't have made it if she hadn't had her sister to lean on.

But now he wanted her to know that she didn't have to be as strong anymore. Not that he was stronger in the sense that he could overpower her or hurt her. He just wanted her to know he was strong enough for her to let go, to trust, to take that leap of faith and truly let another person get close to her.

She was close to her sister, but that wasn't a threat because on a gut-deep level, he realized Cyn knew she was still in charge. If she got as close to him as he wanted her to be, she'd have to relinquish part of the control that was always with her and that defined her life.

He wanted that. Badly.

Oh, she gave over in bed. She was a wonderfully responsive woman. But he wanted more than the physical. Living and working on the ranch, he saw miracles manifest themselves in countless ways. Gracie had been one. He hadn't stopped praying the entire time he'd been in that stall, praying that the mare and her foal would survive that horrible night.

He knew better than to believe that what had happened had really had anything to do with either him or Rose. When you worked with animals, or the land, a Higher Power came into play, and only a fool couldn't acknowledge something that true.

He'd read a lot over the long winters when he'd been alone. Funny, how even with Annie, he'd still felt alone after the first few months. And he knew he believed much the same way the Indians did, that everything was interconnected, everything was consciousness, and must be honored and respected. Including a Higher Power.

Now he turned to that Higher Power, a power his mother had taught him to trust, a power he sensed in the world all the time, wherever he was and whatever he did. His words were simple and from the heart.

Help her to trust me. Please. I may be selfish to ask for such a thing, but I need it. I need to know she's with me. That she trusts me. I need her to give over that terrible sense of control. She has to feel safe enough to do that, I know. I'll wait for her. But if you could give me a little help on this one . . .

He contemplated the stars, the night sky, the wind keening through the trees. He gained strength from the land, and tried as hard as he could to give back, to strike a delicate balance. And now he wanted that balance between him and his wife.

It's not that I won't love her if it never happens. I made that promise the day I married her. Just to love her. And I will, the rest of my life. But help her to see that I'm here for her, and I'm not going to go away like both her parents did. I'll be here for her until the day I die, and even beyond that if what I feel in my heart for this woman is as true as I believe it is....

He sighed. Chance had waited, alone, for a long time before taking his true wife. He'd thought about Rosie. He'd made a mistake with Annie. And he'd known, after the initial emotional and hormonal madness, that he'd been put in that bar in Las Vegas for a reason. That he and Cyn had created a child together for a reason. That what they had was fated to be, and a wise man simply accepted what was given to him.

He'd been given everything when she'd walked through that door. She'd brought him to his knees in the way that only the right woman can. He'd been vulnerable to her, and now he wanted her to stop holding back, to stop playing it safe, to jump into that most romantic and sensual abyss with him.

He smiled, then looked out over the yard toward the stable. Lights were still on in the bunkhouse, and he knew the ranch hands who had stayed on over the holidays were having a wild time.

But they would all be up in the morning, ready to work the land and give back to the natural world that gave so much.

He closed his eyes.

Thank you for giving me a woman who sees the beauty of the land, who loves it and respects it the way I do. I never thought I would have that in this lifetime, and I'm grateful. If I never have any more of Cyn than I have at this moment, it's more than enough. But I'm going to continue to care for her. Love her. And hope...

He went back to bed and took his sleeping wife into his arms. He held her next to his heart, listening to the steady, sweet sound of her breathing for a long time before he dropped off to sleep.

CHANCE LOOKED UP at the sky the morning of December 27 and knew they were in for a blizzard. When you worked the land as long as he had, you could just sort of tell.

He had a lot to do, getting the cattle ready to withstand such a storm, making sure everyone on the ranch was safe. He squared his shoulders and got back to work.

CYN WAS WITH EUNICE in the kitchen when she felt the first sharp pain.

"Oh." She grasped the back of one of the kitchen chairs and sat down.

"Honey? What's wrong?"

"A pain. I think—I think I better sit down for a little bit."

"That's a good idea."

"But the baby's not due—"

"No, she's not, is she. Sit down, honey, here's that warm milk. You'll feel better in a minute. I'll be right back."

EUNICE WENT TO HER BEDROOM and used the phone to dial Chance's beeper. He'd told her to use the device only if it was an emergency, specifically if Cyn went into labor.

As she hung up the phone, the woman muttered, "Get back home, Chance. Your baby's on the way."

BY THE TIME he reached the ranch house, she was on her hands and knees in the family room, and in such pain.

"Chance! Oh God, Chance, stop it, please, stop the pain—" Her face contorted in agony, and he knew the baby was coming hard and fast, and they wouldn't have time for Doc or Rosie or anyone else.

No. Oh, no.

Even as his mind formed the words, he was down on the floor beside her, taking her into his arms, holding her, offering comfort, then getting her to lie down on the new rugs installed in the family room such a short time ago.

"Is Doc? Is Doc..." She was panting between the words, and he knew she needed the comfort of hope.

"I called Doc," he said, which wasn't a lie. But Doc had been out of his office, and would never make it to the ranch the way the snow was blowing outside. He'd barely been able to see his way from the stable to the house.

"Okay. Okay—" Another pain hit her and her body arched in agony. "Chance! Oh, Chance—"

Then she reached out for him, held out her hand, grabbed his, practically crushed it with her fingers, and he saw the look in her eyes. He saw that she'd finally, in the midst of her terrible pain and fear, given over everything to him.

Not like this. Not like this.

"Come on, sweetheart. I'm going to get you all comfortable until the baby comes." He couldn't lie to her, even if she was in no condition to understand his words. He couldn't tell her that Doc was on his way when he would never make it on time.

"I'm okay. I'm okay." The pain must have receded, and now she was taking back control, battling to stay in control, needing it.

He didn't care. He didn't care if she never gave over anything to him again, just as long as she got through this safely. In that moment of intense emotion, Chance even forgot their child as he focused on the woman he loved.

"Come on, baby. Move this way. Let me help you—" He put a folded blanket beneath her hips, then slid her panties off. She was wearing a denim skirt and plaid blouse, and he saw Eunice come into the room with one of Cyn's flannel nightgowns.

"Chance, I'm cold." Her teeth were chattering, and he didn't know if it was reaction or an actual chill. He had to do something.

"Let's change you into something a little more comfortable."

"Okay. Okay." She was as obedient as a small child, and Chance knew how scared she had to be.

Once her nightgown was on, and he'd put thick socks on her feet, he propped her shoulders up on pillows and simply held her hand as the next pain hit. She turned her head into one of the pillows and started to cry. He laid his cheek against hers, then kissed her.

"Baby, I'm here, it'll be all right—"

"Gracie," she whispered. "Gracie."

His heart turned over as he remembered the expression on her face that horrible night in the barn.

"No. Not like that." But he wasn't sure. Women generally had longer labors, and the pains didn't come this fast or this strong. Something might be wrong, for this certainly wasn't a normal labor.

"Will you...will you...hit me over the head and knock me out if I ask...you to?" She bit her lip against the pain, and her face paled.

He held on to her hand as she gripped it tightly, like a lifeline. "It's okay, Cyn. I'm here, and everything's going to be all right."

Not like this, please, not like this. Don't let anything be wrong with her, don't take her away from me. I'll give you anything...just don't hurt her.

"Chance...Chance, I don't think I'm very strong."

"You are, baby, you are. You can get through this, we can get through this. It's going to be okay, and—"

Another pain hit, and her body writhed with the effort of fighting it. He saw the expression on her face, the wildness in her eyes, and his heart contracted.

You want the ranch, you've got it. None of it means a thing if she isn't there to share it with me....

He knew enough about delivering babies to know what to look for. So did Eunice.

"She's not far enough along, Chance. Tell her not to push," Eunice whispered.

Chance doubted Cyn had even heard. Her eyes were closed, her body tensed.

"Cyn? Cyn? Don't push. Not yet. Do you hear me?"

She nodded her head, the motion barely perceptible.

He thought of telling Eunice to try Doc again, but a quick glance out the window forestalled that idea. The snow was coming down thick and fast, and they were in this alone, the two of them, with only Eunice for help.

"Scissors and string, clean towels, a washcloth..." He whispered his needs to the older woman, who was as blessedly efficient as she'd always been.

Then he turned his attention back to his wife, and began to hope for another miracle.

"ALL RIGHT, BABY, I want you to push now."

"I...can't."

She was totally exhausted.

"I need you to try now. For me."

She mouthed words, and he had to lower his face to hers to hear them.

I love you.

"I love you, baby." He pushed the damp hair out of her eyes, then kissed her forehead. "I need you to push for me, and the baby needs you to, too."

That seemed to help focus her. She looked up at him with such love and total, unconditional surrender in her beautiful green eyes that his throat closed. He forced himself to speak.

"Push now, Cyn! Now!"

He'd always known she was a strong woman, but the depth of that strength at this moment humbled him.

"Come on! Push! I can see the baby's head!"

He saw her, straining, biting her lip until it bled.

"One more! Come on! You can do it!"

The head was out, then one shoulder.

"That's it! That's my girl!"

The other shoulder, then their little girl was sliding into his hands, and he and Eunice were cleaning her, then cutting the cord.

He gave the child to Eunice and concentrated on his wife until he was sure she wasn't bleeding abnormally. Only then, when he helped her sit up and put the baby to her breasts, did he finally allow himself to cry.

DOC MACKAY CAME OUT and checked both mother and child the following day, his four-wheel drive making short work of the piles of snow in the drive.

"You did a good job, son," he told Chance after hearing Eunice's telling of yesterday's events. "Kept your head just fine. It sure is different when it's your own wife instead of one of the cattle."

It certainly was.

CYN GLANCED UP as her husband came into the bedroom. She'd just finished nursing Emma Kathleen—named after both their mothers—and was about to put the baby down in the crib she'd asked Chance to move next to their bed.

"I'll take her for a minute," he said, and she waited until he took off his clothes and slid into bed with her before placing his tiny daughter in his arms. Cyn watched as Emma lay contentedly against his muscled chest, her tiny fingers flexing as she drifted off to sleep.

"I wish..." Emotion clogged her throat and she cleared it, then started again. "I wish I could've been that way with you. From the start."

"What way?"

She had a feeling he knew, but needed to hear the words.

"Trusting."

The moment was so charged with emotion, she knew she'd remember it forever.

"Maybe if I'd had you for a father... I'm not making any sense."

"Yes, you are. I understand."

Tears filled her eyes. Were there any two words more beautiful in the English language? And he did understand, and he offered her his total acceptance, which meant the world to her.

"You saved my life."

"Cyn—"

"No. Doc told me some of that wasn't normal. You brought me and Emma through just fine." She was shaking as she cried now, and he shifted their daughter against his chest and enfolded her in his free arm. She buried her face against his shoulder and cried, at the same time finding comfort in the way he felt and smelled. The way he was.

When she finished crying, he carefully put their sleeping daughter in her crib, then came back to bed and took her in his arms.

"Chance?"

"Hmm?"

"I want you to know...I don't feel alone anymore."

He kissed her forehead.

"And not just because of Emma."

"I know."

"Something happened...that night."

She felt his smile against her hair.

"I don't...want to go back to the woman I was before."

"Okay."

"Do you know what I'm saying?"

He kissed her then, and she felt it all the way down to her toes. Not as much in a sexual way, but in a way so powerfully emotional it transcended anything she'd felt before.

"I do."

She smiled, and tears welled up again. He carefully brushed them away.

"So," she said, her voice shaky, "do you think we could start this marriage all over again?"

He looked at her with so much love it stole her breath away.

"I think," he said quietly, "there's nothing in this world I would rather do."

NEW YEAR'S EVE was quiet. Cyn sat in the kitchen with Emma in her arms as Eunice bustled around, making last-minute adjustments to the feast she was creating. Chance had gone into town on some errand or other, but had promised to be home in time for dinner.

Cyn heard booted footsteps at the kitchen door, but nothing prepared her for what happened next.

A woman walked in the door, bundled up against the cold. Cyn's throat constricted painfully as she saw the dark red hair above the long knitted scarf, then that scarf was being unwound and her twin's face came into view.

Then total, utter silence as the sisters looked at each other.

Somehow, Luca and Chance left the room, and Eunice stopped her preparations and quietly faded from view.

"Cyn." Pepper's voice was hushed, her tone absolutely reverent. "She's beautiful."

She didn't know what else to do, so she handed her daughter to her sister. Pepper had already taken her heavy coat off, and now held the baby with a fierce hunger that almost caused Cyn to turn away. Some things were too private.

"Emma Kathleen?" Pepper asked.

"Yeah."

They looked at each other, and each knew the other was thinking of their mother.

"That's nice," Pepper whispered as she returned her attention to the infant's curious face. "Remembering her that way."

They didn't say anything for a time, then Pepper asked, "What was it like?"

Cyn composed herself before she spoke. "It was really bad. Chance got me through it."

"Will you have any more?"

"I don't know. It scares me. Maybe, but not right away."

"She's beautiful."

"You think so?" Cyn could feel her control slipping. She'd dreamed of this moment from first discovering she was pregnant, and now knew it for the gift it was.

"She looks just like you," Pepper whispered.

"And you," Cyn added. "How did you get here?"

"Chance called me. He's a good man. He told me how hard things were for you, and that you . . . needed me."

"I do." And with those two words, Cyn felt the last of her walls come crumbling down. They'd already started to disappear with Chance, and now it was the same with her sister. People were strong in different ways, and she no longer felt she had to take that strength and use it to wall off other people.

It felt so much better, getting close.

"I'm going to go check on Luca," Pepper said, but the heart of her attention was on her tiny niece.

"I will," Cyn said, getting up. "You two get to know each other."

She was almost to the family room when she heard Luca talking to Chance. Spilling out his emotions.

"She won't adopt, she says she can't, and I don't know what we're going to do...."

Not wanting to intrude, she grabbed her jacket from the front closet and let herself out the front door, avoiding both the family room and the kitchen. Eunice would put all the food out soon, and they would celebrate the coming year. But first, she had to do a little soul-searching.

The night was calm, cold and beautifully serene. Her boots crunched through the thin film of ice on top of the packed snow as she walked to one of the corrals and leaned against it. She looked up into the sky and studied the stars.

All her life she'd quietly dreamed, never expecting to get half of what she now possessed. A husband who loved her, a beautiful baby girl. A ranch they would work and pass down to their children. Days filled with hard work and laughter, peacefulness and loving.

Pepper's dreams could never come true.

Help me. Help me see the right way. The right path.

She studied the stars and remembered that first Christmas star, and what one man's sacrifice had ultimately done to change the face of the world.

The idea slipped into her head so quietly, so confidently, that she knew it had been given to her. Another gift in a life so completely blessed. Another miracle.

I can do that.

But would Chance agree? She didn't even hesitate, knowing her husband would understand.

Cyn went back inside. They ate dinner and laughed, talked and joked. Saw in the New Year with much kissing and hugging, and funny resolutions. And afterward, with Emma safely in bed and her entire family under the ranch house's generous roof, Cyn approached her husband and told him what she wanted to do.

He stood behind her, as she knew he would, one hundred percent.

Eighteen months later...

"PUSH, CYN, you can push now. I can see the head." Doc MacKay's voice was calm, yet there was a tinge of excitement to his words. Even after delivering countless babies, he'd told her that such an event never lost its essential magic.

This time the delivery was much easier. Doc had told her that each was different, and she was thankful. Chance stood by her side and held her shoulders as she felt the baby leave her body, and, knowing it was a little boy, she wished him well.

And let him go.

Doc cleaned the little one up and placed the baby in Pepper's arms. She was crying so hard she couldn't stop. Both she and Luca had been present during the entire delivery, but now their focus narrowed to the child Cyn had given them.

The child Pepper and Luca should have had. It had been a simple matter for Cyn to become pregnant through artificial insemination. Now the child that her twin held in her arms was really a part of both her and her husband.

Cyn lay back against her husband's solid chest and watched her twin through her tears.

"No regrets?" Chance asked her softly, his lips brushing her ear.

She knew he meant giving her sister the baby, and she had none about her decision. In a strange way, that little boy had always belonged to Pepper. Cyn had seen him safely into the world and would always be a part of his life, but he was Pepper and Luca's child now, for them to love, cherish and protect.

"Regrets?" She thought back to all she'd been through to get to this exact moment in time, all the twists and turns, the doubts and heartache.

And all the love. Always the love.

She looked up at her husband, her hero, the man who had won both her trust and her heart and would always be a part of her life.

"Not one."

With the advent of spring, American Romance
is pleased to be presenting exciting couples, each
with their own unique reasons for needing a new
beginning...for needing to enter into a marriage
of convenience.

In April we brought you #580 MARRIAGE
INCORPORATED by Debbi Rawlins, and in
May we offered #583 THE RUNAWAY BRIDE
by Jacqueline Diamond. Next, meet the reluctant
newlyweds in:

#587 A SHOTGUN WEDDING
Cathy Gillen Thacker
June 1995

Find out why some couples marry first...and learn to
love later. Watch for the upcoming "In Name Only"
promotion.

ANNOUNCING THE

FLYAWAY VACATION SWEEPSTAKES!

This month's destination:

Beautiful SAN FRANCISCO!

This month, as a special surprise, we're offering an exciting FREE VACATION!

Think how much fun it would be to visit San Francisco "on us"! You could ride cable cars, visit Chinatown, see the Golden Gate Bridge and dine in some of the finest restaurants in America!

The facing page contains two Entry Coupons (as does every book you received this shipment). Complete and return *all* the entry coupons; **the more times you enter, the better your chances of winning!**

Then keep your fingers crossed, because you'll find out by June 15, 1995 if you're the winner! If you are, here's what you'll get:

- Round-trip airfare for two to beautiful San Francisco!
- 4 days/3 nights at a first-class hotel!
- $500.00 pocket money for meals and sightseeing!

Remember: The more times you enter, the better your chances of winning!*

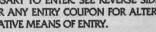

*NO PURCHASE OR OBLIGATION TO CONTINUE BEING A SUBSCRIBER NECESSARY TO ENTER. SEE REVERSE SIDE OR ANY ENTRY COUPON FOR ALTERNATIVE MEANS OF ENTRY.

VSF KAL

FLYAWAY VACATION
SWEEPSTAKES
OFFICIAL ENTRY COUPON

This entry must be received by: MAY 30, 1995
This month's winner will be notified by: JUNE 15, 1995
Trip must be taken between: JULY 30, 1995-JULY 30, 1996

YES, I want to win the San Francisco vacation for two. I understand the prize includes round-trip airfare, first-class hotel and $500.00 spending money. Please let me know if I'm the winner!

Name_____

Address _____ Apt. _____

City   State/Prov.   Zip/Postal Code

Account #_____

Return entry with invoice in reply envelope.

© 1995 HARLEQUIN ENTERPRISES LTD.   CSF KAL

FLYAWAY VACATION
SWEEPSTAKES
OFFICIAL ENTRY COUPON

This entry must be received by: MAY 30, 1995
This month's winner will be notified by: JUNE 15, 1995
Trip must be taken between: JULY 30, 1995-JULY 30, 1996

YES, I want to win the San Francisco vacation for two. I understand the prize includes round-trip airfare, first-class hotel and $500.00 spending money. Please let me know if I'm the winner!

Name_____

Address _____ Apt. _____

City   State/Prov.   Zip/Postal Code

Account #_____

Return entry with invoice in reply envelope.

© 1995 HARLEQUIN ENTERPRISES LTD.   CSF KAL

OFFICIAL RULES

FLYAWAY VACATION SWEEPSTAKES 3449

NO PURCHASE OR OBLIGATION NECESSARY

Three Harlequin Reader Service 1995 shipments will contain respectively, coupons for entry into three different prize drawings, one for a trip for two to San Francisco, another for a trip for two to Las Vegas and the third for a trip for two to Orlando, Florida. To enter any drawing using an Entry Coupon, simply complete and mail according to directions.

There is no obligation to continue using the Reader Service to enter and be eligible for any prize drawing. You may also enter any drawing by hand printing the words "Flyaway Vacation," your name and address on a 3"x5" card and the destination of the prize you wish that entry to be considered for (i.e., San Francisco trip, Las Vegas trip or Orlando trip). Send your 3"x5" entries via first-class mail (limit: one entry per envelope) to: Flyaway Vacation Sweepstakes 3449, c/o Prize Destination you wish that entry to be considered for, P.O. Box 1315, Buffalo, NY 14269-1315, USA or P.O. Box 610, Fort Erie, Ontario L2A 5X3, Canada.

To be eligible for the San Francisco trip, entries must be received by 5/30/95; for the Las Vegas trip, 7/30/95; and for the Orlando trip, 9/30/95.

Winners will be determined in random drawings conducted under the supervision of D.L. Blair, Inc., an independent judging organization whose decisions are final, from among all eligible entries received for that drawing. San Francisco trip prize includes round-trip airfare for two, 4-day/3-night weekend accommodations at a first-class hotel, and $500 in cash (trip must be taken between 7/30/95—7/30/96, approximate prize value—$3,500); Las Vegas trip includes round-trip airfare for two, 4-day/3-night weekend accommodations at a first-class hotel, and $500 in cash (trip must be taken between 9/30/95—9/30/96, approximate prize value—$3,500); Orlando trip includes round-trip airfare for two, 4-day/3-night weekend accommodations at a first-class hotel, and $500 in cash (trip must be taken between 11/30/95—11/30/96, approximate prize value—$3,500). All travelers must sign and return a Release of Liability prior to travel. Hotel accommodations and flights are subject to accommodation and schedule availability. Sweepstakes open to residents of the U.S. (except Puerto Rico) and Canada, 18 years of age or older. Employees and immediate family members of Harlequin Enterprises, Ltd., D.L. Blair, Inc., their affiliates, subsidiaries and all other agencies, entities and persons connected with the use, marketing or conduct of this sweepstakes are not eligible. Odds of winning a prize are dependent upon the number of eligible entries received for that drawing. Prize drawing and winner notification for each drawing will occur no later than 15 days after deadline for entry eligibility for that drawing. Limit: one prize to an individual, family or organization. All applicable laws and regulations apply. Sweepstakes offer void wherever prohibited by law. Any litigation within the province of Quebec respecting the conduct and awarding of the prizes in this sweepstakes must be submitted to the Regies des loteries et Courses du Quebec. In order to win a prize, residents of Canada will be required to correctly answer a time-limited arithmetical skill-testing question. Value of prizes are in U.S. currency.

Winners will be obligated to sign and return an Affidavit of Eligibility within 30 days of notification. In the event of noncompliance within this time period, prize may not be awarded. If any prize or prize notification is returned as undeliverable, that prize will not be awarded. By acceptance of a prize, winner consents to use of his/her name, photograph or other likeness for purposes of advertising, trade and promotion on behalf of Harlequin Enterprises, Ltd., without further compensation, unless prohibited by law.

For the names of prizewinners (available after 12/31/95), send a self-addressed, stamped envelope to: Flyaway Vacation Sweepstakes 3449 Winners, P.O. Box 4200, Blair, NE 68009.

RVC KAL